AF655620

TRAIN TO DELHI

BY THE SAME AUTHOR

The Best of Faiz
Nude before God

TRAIN TO DELHI

A NOVEL

SHIV K. KUMAR

PENGUIN BOOKS
An imprint of Penguin Random House

PENGUIN BOOKS

USA | Canada | UK | Ireland | Australia
New Zealand | India | South Africa | China | Singapore

Penguin Books is part of the Penguin Random House group of companies whose addresses can be found at global.penguinrandomhouse.com

Published by Penguin Random House India Pvt. Ltd
4th Floor, Capital Tower 1, MG Road,
Gurugram 122 002, Haryana, India

Penguin Random House India

First published in 1998 as *A River with Three Banks, The Partition of India: Agony and Ecstasy* by UBS Publishers' Distributors Pvt Ltd, New Delhi
Published by Random House India in 2013

This edition published in Penguin Books by Penguin Random House India 2020

All rights reserved

10 9 8 7 6 5 4 3 2

This is a work of fiction. Names, characters, places and incidents are either the product of the author's imagination or are used fictitiously and any resemblance to any actual person, living or dead, events or locales is entirely coincidental.

ISBN 9788184003963

Typeset in Sabon by R. Ajith Kumar

Printed at Repro India Limited

This book is sold subject to the condition that it shall not, by way of trade or otherwise, be lent, resold, hired out, or otherwise circulated without the publisher's prior consent in any form of binding or cover other than that in which it is published and without a similar condition including this condition being imposed on the subsequent purchaser.

www.penguin.co.in

FSC www.fsc.org MIX Paper from responsible sources FSC® C047271

This is a legitimate digitally printed version of the book and therefore might not have certain extra finishing on the cover.

To
my father
Late Shri Bishan Das Kumar

1

It was the quietest day of the week—comparatively speaking, of course. Only one death reported in the press: 'a member of the minority community' shot by 'some unknown person', from a speeding jeep, near the Red Fort. Although censorship had sternly warned all media against attributing such killings to any community, it was never difficult to guess which community had committed any particular crime. From the report of the solitary killing that morning, it was, for instance, clear that some helpless Muslim had been gunned down by a fanatic Hindu in yet another act of vendetta for what the Hindus and Sikhs in Pakistan had suffered. But now it seemed as though, after a hectic spell of arson, rape and massacre, Delhi was gradually winding down—at least for a short while.

So when free India voluntarily chose to install Lord Louis Mountbatten as its first governor-general, it was commented that it desperately needed the guidance of this member of the British royalty to help it set up an effective administrative machinery. But he soon became so popular that he was nicknamed 'Pandit Mountbatten'. On the other hand, many Indian gossip columnists played up a different story. According to them, Lady Edwina Mountbatten had a crush on Pandit Jawaharlal Nehru, for didn't this fair-complexioned, Harrow-Cambridge-educated man also look like a prince? So, the least Nehru could do for his lady-love's husband was to offer the top position in an independent India.

But neither Mountbatten nor Nehru—nor even Mahatma Gandhi—could restrain the Hindu and Sikh refugees who had fled from the newly created nation, Pakistan, and who were now lusting for Muslim blood.

In the early afternoon of that quiet day, a young man in a light grey suit was dropped by a taxi at the mouth of a narrow street. He began to jostle his way through a crowd of shoppers who were picking up their groceries before another curfew would immobilize life in the capital.

There wasn't much of a rush further down the street where a few refugee vendors had spread their wares: coarse woollens (sweaters, stoles, stockings, gloves), necklaces and bracelets in coloured beads, and tiny bronze gods and goddesses. Behind a low wooden table used as a bargain counter, a vendor's young wife was feeding her little infant, her moist, right nipple showing through her partly unbuttoned choli, as her husband held up an idol of Lord Shiva to a lanky, indifferent customer whose eyes had meandered towards the young mother's ripe breast. The young man in the grey suit also glanced at the woman, but he didn't stop. Anxiety rippled all over his face. Emerging at the other end of the street, he turned sharply round a corner and strode towards a cathedral. He paused at its front gate for a moment, flicked a speck of dust off his jacket, then trudged across a vast courtyard towards the bishop's residence. Even before his hand could reach the call-bell, the door opened as though reflexively, and a white man in a crisp silken robe peered out.

'Mr Gautam Mehta?' he inquired, raising his right hand as if in benediction.

'Yes, Father.'

'Come in, please.'

Gautam Mehta took in the bishop at a glance. He was a medium-statured, stocky man in his late fifties—a sallow face, bulbous nose, sagging jaw, sea-blue eyes, and high cheekbones. The hair on his head was sparse; in fact, a round patch of baldness showed just above the forehead. But what held Gautam's immediate attention was a pair of hands—white, soft and sensitive—hands that must have been moulded by years of prayerful posture in offerings of love, compassion and forgiveness.

The bishop led his visitor through the drawing room to his study, a small oval-shaped room stacked with books. On the front wall hung a large canvas of a wounded Christ lying on Virgin Mary's lap. Jesus's face, petulant and confused, looked like that of a soccer centre forward knocked off his feet near the goal. Gautam wondered if the painting had been done by some novice pavement artist. In a corner stood a small aquarium filled with Chinese goldfish, frisking about in limpid, blue water.

Pointing to a padded leather chair, the bishop said, 'Won't you sit down?'

'Thank you,' replied Gautam.

The bishop himself took his seat in a swivel chair.

'It's much quieter here,' said the bishop. 'I guess the city is calm today.'

'Yes, Father.'

'I hope it stays so.'

'I hope so too.'

'But one never knows.'

'No, Father.'

A white cat with black whiskers slunk into the room, stared pointedly at the visitor, then glided sinuously towards the bishop, who took it up on his lap and began caressing the nape of its neck, his mobile fingers running up and down its fluffy back. Purring, the cat closed its eyes, as though in serene composure.

'A very pretty cat,' Gautam remarked, more as an ingratiating gesture than out of any appreciation of the animal's beauty.

'Yes, Belinda is just adorable.' The bishop paused. 'Would you care for a soft drink, Mr Mehta—lemonade or pineapple?'

'Please don't bother.'

'Do have something. It's a scorching day.'

'A lemonade then, please.'

With Belinda under his arm, the bishop disappeared into the house. Gautam heard him asking his servant for two lemonades. It was a gracious voice, as if the bishop were seeking a favour. Gautam somehow felt assured of the success of his mission though his face was still tensed up.

No, he told himself, he mustn't give himself away. He must summon his memory, quote promptly and aptly from the Bible to pull off what he had in mind. For the past one week, he had given the book the same close study that a medical student would give to Gray's *Anatomy*.

Still holding the cat, Father Jones returned to his chair,

followed by a dark man carrying two lemonades on a china tray.

'Thank you,' Gautam said, taking one glass from the tray.

'Thank you, Samuel,' said the bishop, putting down Belinda in order to take the other glass.

Just as the servant withdrew, the bishop swivelled in his chair, and pulled out an envelope from the top drawer of his rosewood desk. Waving it in his right hand, he said: 'Maybe if you'd telephoned me, we could have at least talked before . . .' His voice trailed off. 'You see, I got nothing out of your letter.'

If the bishop's tone had not been genial, Gautam would have felt somewhat rattled.

'I'm sorry, Father,' said Gautam. 'Since writing, I guess, comes more naturally to me than speaking, I thought I'd rather send you a letter.'

'Oh yes,' the bishop responded with a gleam of understanding in his sea-blue eyes. 'Incidentally, isn't your paper a bit too radical—secular? That's what I'm told. I don't read it myself though.'

'I'm responsible only for the literary section—stories, reviews, poetry and miscellaneous articles. Sometimes I myself do a piece on the cultural scene in Delhi. Only last week, I wrote something on tolerance and non-violence. Almost a sermon.'

'Sounds good.' The bishop's face returned to its pristine glow, as though his mind had been cleared of some dark cobweb. After a brief silence, he added, 'I'm happy you've decided to come to Christ, voluntarily. Not many people would do that, you know. Was your decision . . .'

Gautam had anticipated the question Father Jones was finding difficult to articulate. He moved in promptly.

'It's not easy, Father, to explain these matters of the spirit and heart. Perhaps I should just say that I've felt, all these years, an irrepressible urge . . .' He paused, taking the bishop's measure. 'Maybe it started when I was just an undergraduate, with my interest in Cardinal Newman, then with other Catholic writers—Francois Mauriac, Evelyn Waugh, Graham Greene . . .'

Gautam was pleased with his well-rehearsed speech, and more pleased to notice Father Jones lapping it up.

'Yes, I understand,' Father Jones said, drawling out the last word.

'And then,' Gautam was now warming up to his subject, 'look at what my co-religionists are doing these days. All this pious talk about Brahma, ahimsa, the Higher Self, cow worship, and then this senseless killing of innocent Muslims! Of course, Muslims have done no better in Pakistan.'

'It's all very sad.'

'Yes, very tragic. Don't you see, Father, that Christians alone have kept their heads cool?' He glanced at the bishop for approval. 'I believe in karma,' he continued, 'concrete action—not just words.'

Belinda, who'd hunched up on the floor near the bishop's chair, suddenly craned its neck forward, riveting its burnt sienna eyes on Gautam's face. For a moment he thought that the beautiful, perceptive animal had seen right through him.

'Yes,' said the bishop, nodding at Gautam's words; then, after a moment's pause, he added: 'I hope you wouldn't mind waiting a couple of months. I have in mind the usual process of initiation—Bible classes, seminars, catechism. Sort of a religious apprenticeship, you know. Literature is one thing,' he looked directly at Gautam, 'but the Book of Books is something entirely different.'

Gautam's face darkened. The mere thought of any delay was agonizing. If only this man knew what he'd been through. To hell with Hinduism, Islam or Christianity, he said to himself—all that he wanted was an instant release, a way out of this labyrinth, a quick, painless deliverance.

'But, Father, haven't I already waited long enough?' he asked. 'What about all those years of apprenticeship?' He decided to fire his first biblical shot: 'I was hoping that when I knocked at the door, it would open unto me.'

The bishop was taken aback, but he quickly recovered.

'Haste in such matters, Mr Mehta, is not good. In any case, shouldn't you have brought your wife along too? It would have saved time for you both.'

'I'd thought of that,' Gautam answered, sensing now a loss of initiative. 'But, unfortunately, she still seems to have reservations. It's her orthodox Hindu background, I guess.'

He broke off, hoping to regain his self-possession. 'But, Father,' he resumed, 'isn't an unbelieving wife converted through her husband? Isn't that what Paul is getting at in Corinthians?'

Surely, Father Jones now realized that this man knew his Bible intimately.

Belinda, who'd glided across the floor to the door, darted another searching glance at Gautam. It was an uncanny stare that almost chilled him.

'Yes, that's what he intended,' said the bishop. 'But I

should like to avoid any discord in the family—as far as possible.'

'No discord whatsoever,' Gautam said, still recovering from the eerie spell of Belinda's gaze. 'In fact, we've talked about this matter, and I feel she's gradually coming around.'

'Good.'

'It's just that I shouldn't like to push . . .'

'No coercion, please,' Father Jones interjected. 'We should come to the Lord only out of the freedom and power of our soul. Like yourself.'

'Precisely.'

Gautam turned to Belinda, but her gaze was now riveted on the aquarium, where it observed one goldfish furiously chasing another.

'Well, Mr Mehta,' the bishop said, drawing a deep breath, 'if that's the case, we should perhaps go ahead without any delay. I have no right to keep you away from the Lord.' He stopped to look straight at Gautam. 'How about next Sunday? We would have a special service for you so that the entire congregation could bless you.'

Gautam was shocked. Any such public ceremony would be a disaster. Being a journalist himself, the press would surely pick it up. He'd hoped instead for a quiet, private ceremony on some weekday, with only two or three people in attendance. The certificate of baptism was all that he wanted to grab. That was his passport to freedom. But, despite the bishop's disconcerting suggestion, he resolved to keep cool.

'Certainly,' he replied, smiling. 'You may do it any time, Father . . .' he paused, glancing at the bishop, 'but, I have always felt that true prayer is strictly a private affair, an intimate communication between man and God—something done in the silence and tranquillity of one's soul.' Suddenly, he brightened up, as though a divine prompter had offered him the master cue. 'Remember the passage in Matthew, Father?'

'Which passage?'

'Yes,' he said, pressing his forehead with his fingers as if to extract some words from the deep reservoir of his memory. 'Yes,' he repeated, 'I have the words: 'and when you pray, you must not be like the hypocrites, for they love to stand and pray in synagogues and at the street corners, that they may be seen by men . . . But when you pray, go into your room, and shut the door and pray to your Father who is in secret, and your Father who sees in secret will reward you.' Gautam paused for a moment, then added, with a complacent smile, 'I don't think I've missed a word.'

'You certainly know your Bible!'

'I wonder,' he said. 'It's just that this passage has always been my favourite.'

'That was a noble thought,' the bishop said. 'The Lord alone can look into the deepest recesses of your soul.'

Belinda slunk out of the room, as though crestfallen, for hadn't it lost some mysterious battle to Gautam?

Picking up his diary, the bishop resumed: 'Would next Thursday be all right? We'll make it a brief and quiet affair.'

'Thank you, Father.'

'But you'll have to bring someone along as your witness.'

'I will.'

Just as Gautam stood up to leave, an outburst of shouting blared in from the street. Then came the clamour of frenetic knocking at the front gate, accompanied by ear-piercing cries for help. But a menacing voice slashed the air: 'Kill him! Har Har Mahadev!' followed by another deafening yell: 'Sat Sri Akal!'

Instantly, some members of the church staff—junior priests, wardens and servants—rushed into the courtyard. Father Jones and Gautam also ran towards the gate. Pounding upon the gate, someone was trying to crash through. Just then a head loomed above it, a poignant cry exploding in the air: 'Help me, please, h-e-l-p!' A man was struggling to scale the gate. But each time his head surfaced, his feet slipped and he sank to the ground. The steel gate stood firm, impregnable.

As thc church warden unlatched the gate, there slumped on the floor the body of an old bearded man—his chest, neck and abdomen riddled with stab wounds. His intestines lay sprawling about. Gazing at the dead body, Gautam felt as though the man was staring back at him, in stark terror.

Two of the bloodthirsty mob's ringleaders looked momentarily at the bishop. Then, as though overawed by the dignity of this Englishman, they beckoned their followers to move on.

'Oh Jesus!' Father Jones exclaimed, crossing his chest with his right hand. 'Is it another crucifixion?' he muttered in anguish. Then, turning to Gautam, he added: 'This man knocked frantically for admittance, but we couldn't let him in.'

'Would that have really helped?' Gautam said. 'We're dealing with bloodhounds, not human beings.'

'Maybe you're right,' the bishop said, looking at the dead body. 'I wonder who this unfortunate creature is.'

This prompted to action his servant, Samuel, who had till now stood aghast. Gently, he began to pull the body across the gate into the courtyard. Then he turned it over, rummaging through the pockets of the dead man's blood-stained jacket, from one of which he pulled out an envelope, stamped and addressed, as though the man had just stepped out to mail it. Samuel handed it over to his master who, after opening it, passed it on to Gautam.

'Urdu, I guess,' said the bishop. 'Do you know this language?'

'Yes, Father.'

The letter was addressed to Sultana Begum, wife of Abdul Rahim, Mohalla Kashana, Aghapura, Allahabad. Taking the letter in his hand, Gautam read out a quick rendering in English, in a voice that was heavy and tremulous:

> Dear Begum,
>
> No trace of Haseena so far. I've been all over Delhi. Hindus and Sikhs are prowling about everywhere, thirsting for Muslim blood. I have to be wary because of my beard, which attracts prying eyes. But so far Allah has been my protector.
>
> This morning I talked to a Muslim shopkeeper in Urdu Bazaar, near Jama Masjid. I was shocked to learn that most of the girls abducted from Allahabad, Lucknow and Patna have been brought to Delhi, where they are forced into prostitution. O Allah! And, in this nefarious business, both Hindus and Muslims are operating as close accomplices. I shudder to think of our dear child.

Spent all morning in Jama Masjid—on my knees, rubbing my nose against the sacred ground. Will Allah listen to my prayers?

Shall write to you tomorrow again. Insha Allah, after meeting this shopkeeper. He has promised to put me in touch with one of the leading pimps, Suleiman Ghani. I may have to pay a heavy ransom to get Haseena out, if she's still alive . . .

Oh God: Don't let Salma stir out anywhere.
Sometimes I wonder why our British rulers chose to leave us to these Hindu bloodsuckers.
God be with you all!

Abdul

The letter stunned Father Jones. So deeply was he moved that moisture welled up in his eyes. Was it the legacy of the Original Sin? Oh Christ, how could he endure all this? Evil was rampant everywhere. There was no help.

'Will you write to his wife, please?' he turned to Gautam. 'Tell her . . .' But his voice broke down. He stood staring at the dead man.

The bishop had been in India for only six months, but was now witnessing this communal holocaust. No, he would not forsake his flock here. Hadn't God preordained his staying on—to do his duty unto Christ? If he now ran away with his other compatriots, who would reclaim lost souls—like Mehta's?

As Father Jones stood transfixed, deeply immersed in his musings, Gautam gazed at the dead man, whose face had acquired a new eloquence in the light of his poignant letter.

Suddenly, he recognized a striking resemblance between Abdul Rahim and his own father—the same wheatish complexion, arched eyebrows, chiselled chin and nose. A handsome face, altogether.

'So, it hasn't turned out to be a calm day, after all.' Father Jones said, in an almost self-derisive tone.

'No.'

'How sadly mistaken we both were.'

'Yes, Father.'

'This may trigger off another round of violence.'

'Most likely.'

Again the bishop's eyes strayed towards the dead man.

'Shouldn't we inform the police?' he asked Gautam.

'But would it serve any purpose? I'm certain they're in league with these killers. They move in much after all is over.'

'Then there is no law and order.'

'No. Delhi's only hope is William Thornton, our commissioner of police. But what can a single man do?'

'Thornton? An Englishman?' asked Father Jones.

'No, Anglo-Indian. Father English, mother Kashmiri.'

'I see,' the bishop murmured. 'I'm glad you were with me this afternoon.'

'But do you realize, Father, what you are doing for me?'

'I don't know. Let Christ be with you hereafter—let him guide your steps.' His voice was a murmur; then it rose: 'Be careful, Mr Mehta, as you go home. There's madness on the streets.'

'No harm will come to me since I live in a Hindu locality.'

'That's good,' the bishop said. 'Then, until Thursday.'

Turning to Samuel, he now asked him to have the dead body removed for a burial in the backyard of the church.

As Gautam walked out of the church into the street, he was surprised to see all quiet everywhere. Where had the rioters disappeared? Or had the police warned them to stay away so that the law could stage a sham investigation into the killing?

Once out on the street, fear suddenly gripped him. What if he was ambushed by some Muslims? He felt as though the dead man's eyes were following him.

He kept on walking, engrossed in his thoughts. Down the street, all the vendors had folded up their stalls. The entire place had been taken over by armed policemen who moved about cockily, brandishing their neatly polished batons.

Near the Red Fort there was no taxi, only a solitary tonga, with a hefty Sikh perched on the front seat. Gautam thought it safe to take this vehicle, with a sturdy Sardar as his escort.

'Can you take me to Darya Ganj, please—Hindu sector?' asked Gautam.

The driver shot a glance at Gautam, his blood-red eyes glistening even in the evening light.

'Yes, but only via the Jumna route,' the Sikh grunted. He then spat vigorously, his spittle landing on the far end of the pavement. 'I think there's trouble near the southern end of Faiz Bazaar.'

Gautam understood it was only a ruse to touch him for more money.

'All right.'

'Fifteen rupees.'

'Okay. Let's go.'

As the rickety vehicle, pulled by a shaggy horse, jerked into a rattle on the road, the driver started a friendly conversation, as a palliative for the exorbitant fare he'd hooked out of his passenger.

'Are you a refugee from Pakistan, sir?'

'Yes—from Lahore.'

'Lost everything?'

'Only property—my family came through, intact.'

'Were you with your family in Lahore, sir?'

'No, I'd come to Delhi a couple of years earlier.'

'Lucky,' he said, his face turning ashen. 'My family had the worst of it . . . Two of my sisters were carried away. My old man's throat was slit before my mother's eyes. Then he was roasted alive. I was the only one to escape. Oh, those blasted Muslims!'

'I'm sorry to hear this.'

'But we got one Muslim this afternoon, near St. John's. An old bearded fellow. That was a good catch.'

'Yes, I know.'

Gautam wondered if the Sardar was himself one of the killers of Abdul Rahim.

2

Darya Ganj lies sprawling like the stomach of Delhi whose head is the Central Secretariat raised in red sandstone, and whose legs and feet taper off into the Delhi University campus, and the refugee colony known as the Kingsway Camp. Delhi's vast belly covers about a square mile between the Delhi Gate and the Red Fort, its intestines coiling round a multitude of narrow streets and bylanes running on either side of Faiz Bazaar, which acts as a watershed between the two belligerent communities, Hindu and Muslim, sworn to eternal enmity.

Along one side of Faiz Bazaar are the prosperous Hindu establishments—banks, clinics, restaurants, bookshops and insurance companies. Behind this forefront lie bungalows and multi-storeyed apartments, owned or rented by the Hindu staff attatched mostly to various offices on the main road. Tucked away in the hinterland of this residential area are the regional offices of *The Times of India* and its allied publications.

Nearby, are a couple of three-star hotels (though in respect of service and amenities they could be ranked starless), which cater to the lower middle-class clientele.

Farther, in the rear, is a lacklustre street that runs parallel to the main road. It is cluttered with grubby bakeries, slipshod general stores, wayside tea-stalls and private coaching institutes.

The original town-planners had indeed provided a few parks between complexes of apartments, but these are now rarely frequented by the local residents because of heaps of garbage that lie stinking there.

Although the rear segment of this part of Darya Ganj is walled in by a battered, historic rampart, it offers no protection whatsoever against burglars at night or trespassers during day. Under its fractured cupolas now sleep at night beggars, pickpockets and daily-wage earners.

In contrast with the affluence of the Hindu sector, the other sector, inhabited by Muslims, looks rather impoverished. There are no banks or bookshops here, only petty stalls of tobacconists, book-binders and vegetable sellers. A small dilapidated mosque, sooty and unplastered, offers some religious solace to the Muslims of this area.

The only redeeming feature of this side of Faiz Bazaar is a large restaurant, Neel Kamal, whose cuisine is a great attraction for the entire capital. Although owned by a Hindu refugee from Pakistan, it draws its patrons from all communities—Hindus, Sikhs, Christians, Parsis and even Muslims.

Neel Kamal's hospitality is limitless. It offers its patrons everything—'wine, women and song'—to use an apt cliché. No wonder, it is also a hang-out for pimps, who can be seen nearby at the tobacconist's stall. One of them may ask you genially if you'd be interested in 'some good stuff—virgin or married, Hindu or Muslim.'

For the customers of modest means, or those who prefer an open-air romantic setting for a brief fling, there are the historical ruins known as Kotla Feroze Shah, just a few yards away from the Delhi Gate. Or, if you could spend a little money, you may hire a room for any part of the day or night at the Bridge Hotel, a subsidiary of Neel Kamal, next to the Kotla ruins.

It was a roundabout tonga ride via Kotla Feroze Shah, where the Sikh tonga driver stopped, hoping to pick up an additional passenger or two. Since there was nobody on the road at that time, he poked the horse's behind with a bamboo stick, then lashed him into a canter, shouting a Punjabi abuse: 'You impotent bastard, fit only to sleep with your mother!' As though insulted and injured, the animal broke into a gallop, raced past the Delhi Gate police station, till it was reined in near Neel Kamal. Here, Gautam paid off the driver and waited for a long column of military trucks to rumble past before he could cross the road.

At a quarter past seven, the daylight still lingered nostalgically over the housetops. It appeared as if the sun had gradually withdrawn all its advance pennons at the day's end. In a few minutes, the sky was covered with a medley of dull orange, hectic crimson and murky grey. But, in spite of the shades of evening, the heat still held the capital in its relentless grip. There had hardly been any rain during the entire month of August, as though nature had deliberately smothered the monsoons to provide a grim backdrop to the drama of hate and violence being enacted in Delhi, during that cataclysmic year—1947.

As the last truck rolled past, Gautam strode across the

road. He wondered if he would have time even for a brief word with his wife, Sarita. If the commissioner of police decided to clamp a curfew as a punitive action for the wanton killing near St. John's, Gautam would surely be stuck in Darya Ganj for the night.

To console himself against any such eventuality, he reasoned that a prompt and ruthless administrator like William Thornton wouldn't have waited this long to strike. If he could post armed police around the Red Fort area within minutes of the killing, he would have also ordered a curfew without any delay. No, Mr Thornton had wisely refrained from creating a panic in this part of the capital, over an isolated incident.

After sorting out his thoughts under a lamp post, Gautam walked slowly down a street and stopped in front of a bungalow—his own home until about a week ago. But now he was about to enter it, almost like a burglar, to confront his wife. Yes, Sarita was still his spouse till he got his divorce, and the conversion certificate was the key to his release. 'That Mr Mehta,' his lawyer was never tired of repeating, 'is the only respectable and expeditious way out. All that your wife has to say in the court is that you're now a Christian. And that entitles her to a divorce. Otherwise, the Hindu law is a vicious python that never slackens its clasp.'

A gentle knock at the door evoked a brusque response.

'Who's there?'

The voice was unmistakably Purnima's; but no sound of footsteps was heard down the hallway.

Waiting for the maidservant to show up, his eyes caught the nameplate, nailed above the mailbox: 'Gautam

Mehta, Assistant Editor, *The Challenge*'. It would soon be removed, he guessed, now that he had surrendered the house as a part of the divorce deal. Then he began to gaze idly at the door—at the grains of its teakwood panels till he was deeply absorbed in the figure of a fish staring at him out of the wood. Strange, he mused, he'd never noticed it before. As he let his right hand run over the panel, as if to feel the fish's contours, he suddenly flinched as a globule of blood oozed out of the tip of his forefinger. Pulling out the splinter which had stuck into it, he wiped off the blood with his left thumb. He'd better not touch anything in the house any more, he cautioned himself.

Only last week, he'd chanced upon a greeting card, hidden away in an old copy of *Good Housekeeping* (oh, the irony of it!): 'On our son's second birthday. Love: Mohinder.' He'd then felt as if he'd been pushed into a deep crater of seething lava.

And how stupid of him, his thoughts ran on, to have taken lightly the argument between Sarita and the gynaecologist, the former insisting that her pregnancy was only seven months. Hadn't she computed her periods most meticulously? Asking him to bed the very night he'd returned from Singapore so that her menstrual chronograph might start ticking straightaway! While, in fact, Rahul had emerged a full nine-month, chubby boy, on the auspicious Diwali evening. A special gift from Lord Rama—and from Mohinder, his colleague and friend! And all this time he'd loved Rahul as his own child.

Then came the defiant words, ringing into his ears: 'So what! If you want a divorce, I'll let you have it. Any time!'

The tape had run itself out. How many times during the

past week he'd been ambushed by these horrid memories?

Suddenly, he realized that he had stood at the door a long time, waiting for Purnima. He wondered how much this woman knew about the affair between Sarita and Mohinder.

He gave the door another knock.

'How do you do, Mr Mehta?'

Someone greeted him from across the street. Turning round, he saw Padamnath Trivedi, who lived in the house opposite.

'How do you do, Mr Trivedi? I'm sorry I didn't notice you.'

'Well, I haven't seen you for quite some time—almost a week now.'

The prying devil must have kept a diary to record all his comings and goings, Gautam said to himself. Would he also know anything about his wife's love affair?

'I was out of town,' said Gautam.

A tenuous lie, he thought, should throw him off the scent.

'Is everything all right with you, Mr Mehta?'

The man now strode towards him, itching for a chat. But, fortunately, a face now peered out of the door.

'Sorry, sir, to have kept you waiting so long,' Purnima said, looking quite surprised. 'Someone had just brought in the news about a killing near the Red Fort. So we were terrified to open the door to strangers.'

'Yes, I understand.'

Then came another voice, harsh as a matron's.

'Is it Gautam? . . . At this late hour?'

Two pairs of eyes now glowered at each other.

3

Gautam followed Sarita into his own house, like an unwelcome visitor, while Purnima walked away to her own room. But the maidservant kept her window half-open to see and hear everything. She knew there'd been an explosive confrontation now—something she'd missed for about a week. As Sarita was leading him down the hallway, she fired her first salvo: 'What has brought you here at this hour? You know, the radio has just announced curfew at ten.'

'Oh, I didn't know,' he mumbled, somewhat surprised. So the invincible Thornton had lost his nerve—for once. But what really alarmed him was the menacing thing that now loomed in front of him. Her thundering voice had already knocked him off. But, pulling himself together somehow, he added: 'I just wanted to have a brief word with you.' Gautam almost stuttered.

'Spit it out, will you?' She shot at him again. But before Gautam could even open his mouth, she turned around. 'Or, maybe, you better wait for me in the drawing room till I put Rahul to sleep.'

'Yes,' he said, meekly.

Sitting alone in the drawing room, he looked all around—and mused. This was the house he'd designed himself, the architect hardly making any modifications. Behind this room, detached from the main house, was his study where he could retreat to work in peace and solitude (though he'd soon realized that even the intervening fourteen-inch walls were not quite soundproof against his wife's ceaseless hollering). On the other side were two bedrooms—one had been furnished as Rahul's nursery, while the other . . .

But he suddenly felt as though his heart had missed a beat. There, in *his* bed, Mohinder and his wife must have played together, night after night, while he was abroad. Since this bedroom lay in the farthest corner of the house, behind the front verandah, her lover must have found it convenient to walk in and out, unobtrusively, any time.

No, he jerked himself out of his reverie; he shouldn't sink into these gruesome thoughts—that way lay insanity. He wouldn't then be able to face the divorce proceedings. This streak of effeminacy, this lapsing into melancholia, could be his undoing. Look at this woman, he told himself. She fights back with complete sangfroid. No sniffling, no wavering, no regrets. That's the way to do it, man.

Suddenly, little Rahul toddled into the drawing room, followed by Sarita. So the child must have heard his voice.

'Daddy!' he cried out gleefully, his eyes still drowsy.

Gautam picked him up gently on his lap, and kissed him on the left cheek. Since he'd always loved him as his own, how could he now disown him? It would be very heart-rending—even though he saw the imprint of Mohinder's features etched indelibly on the child's face.

'Put him down, will you?' snarled Sarita. 'You don't have to impress me with your magnanimity.'

'I wasn't trying to impress . . .'

'Never mind . . . We don't have much time, you know.'

She pulled the child away, and sat on the sofa, facing Gautam squarely. Rahul shrank on his mother's lap, dazed and terrified.

She had now done her hair in a bun at the nape of her neck, looking rather attractive in her pink Kanchivaram sari. A translucent matching blouse partly revealed her breasts. A stray curl dangled casually near her left ear. Gautam also noticed a diamond nose ring. A gift from Mohinder? Why had she taken so long to dress herself for the confrontation? Did she want to show that she was still young and beautiful, capable of taking care of herself?

'I just came to tell you about my meeting with the bishop,' Gautam now said, his voice almost a whisper.

'Oh, the certificate!'

'Yes.'

'I thought you were to meet him tomorrow.'

'No, it was today.'

Then, fixing him with a cold stare, she said: 'You certainly sound excited. It looks as though you've pulled it off.'

He felt the stab of her irony.

'Well, he asked me to meet him again on Thursday, this time along with a witness.'

'Marvellous!' she exclaimed. 'And the witness, I imagine, would be your Berry.'

Gautam thought it discreet to let this one pass too.

After a brief pause, she resumed: 'I guess your father knows about it.'

'Naturally.'

'And he too is excited about it,' she grinned, 'naturally.'

'I don't think so . . . he's only reconciled . . .'

'Such a convenient conscience—of that staunch Arya Samajist.' She broke into such derisive laughter that Rahul felt frightened. He slipped out of her lap and walked away. 'What about his orthodox Hinduism? How does he feel at the prospect of fathering a blooming new-fangled Christian? Maybe his dedication to Swami Dayanand, to the Satyarath Prakash and the Gita was all a sham. Ah, the hypocrite!'

Gautam's first impulse was to shout back at her. But at once he realized that any retaliation at this point would only seal his destiny. If she still chose to deny him the divorce, he'd be bound to the wheel of fire forever. What if she had so wantonly insulted his father? Maybe that was also a part of the price he had to pay for his release.

'I request you to spare my old man—whom you used to call Dad until a few days ago.'

'One Dad's enough for anyone,' she snapped, 'and I have my own.'

She'd indeed worked herself up. But, no, he mustn't hit back. Keep cool, man, he counselled himself. He recalled his meeting with Father Jones, and the vision of imminent release acted as an antidote to this woman's venom.

Sarita noticed him looking at his watch restlessly. It boosted her ego to see him sitting there, utterly humiliated.

'I'd better get moving before I get trapped in the curfew.'

'Yes, and be careful. There are rioters prowling about

everywhere. There may be a retaliation from the Muslim sector any time.'

As she spoke these words, Gautam caught a sinister gleam in her eyes as though she inwardly wished him dead. Wouldn't that be a godsend for her? If only the radio would announce, in an hour or so, that 'a member of the majority community, a journalist, had been stabbed to death near Neel Kamal by some unknown person!'

As for himself, he remembered how, a few months ago, he had seen a cobra under the lemon tree in the backyard, and how he'd chased it across the casuarina hedge. Maybe the reptile was still somewhere around. His mind conjured up a scene—Sarita standing near the tree; a piercing cry, then silence.

'You may now return to your dear father,' she jibed. 'The charter of freedom awaits you at St. John's—next Thursday.'

Suddenly something flashed through his mind. He must make sure that this woman wouldn't do a somersault, and back out of the divorce.

'Look Sarita, we shouldn't wrangle any more,' he said, in a general tone. 'It doesn't do either of us any good . . .' He paused. 'I wish I could tell you something . . . But I don't know how you'd take it.'

'What's it?' Her curiosity was stirred.

'I don't really hate you,' he started off. 'I wish I could open out my heart to you. There's my grievous hurt, of course . . . and Rahul's predicament . . . But won't you agree that we've also had our moments of tenderness . . . If now I ask for divorce, it's because I feel we should live separately for a couple of years so that we may learn to miss each other . . . You know, I have seriously considered remarrying you after . . .'

'The divorce?' Sarita cut in. 'Come, come. Don't you try to fool me.'

But even though Sarita had lapsed into sarcasm, Gautam sensed a ring of confusion in her voice, as though she were pondering over what she'd just heard.

'Please listen—for just a moment.' Gautam came on again. He felt like an actor who, after his prompter's timely cue, doesn't want to be interrupted. The words flowed on, effortlessly.

'Sarita, you may not believe it and, of course, you have the right to distrust me. But, please. . . has it been only hell these four years? Well, if a woman goes astray, it's as much the husband's fault as hers. No, I can't absolve myself of my share of the blame. The child is not mine, I know, but isn't he still as dear to me as if he were? I don't know how to explain . . .'

As he trailed off, he watched Sarita dart a searching glance at his face. He could see that his words had somehow touched her deeply. She was now lost in some introspection.

'Are you putting me on?' she said. But there was no tinge of irony this time, only a feeble urge to fathom the truth.

'Why don't you look into your own soul for the answer?'

Gautam knew that rhetoric could often accomplish much more than a mere statement—and his words had silenced her. Sitting there on the sofa, she was swallowing the bait. She was aware that he couldn't live alone very long—he'd always been such a puny, dependent thing. She was certain he would last only a couple of months. And if he returned to her, vanquished and penitent, shouldn't she accept him? She'd had her fling with Mohinder, but she had never seriously considered marrying him. Marriage was a different thing altogether. Also, Gautam might really adopt Rahul as his own child. Yes, he really loved him. Wasn't Gautam something of a fool too? And all fools, she knew, were capable of spurts of magnanimity. So, let him have the divorce.

As she sat there, lost in her thoughts, Gautam felt convinced that she'd swallowed the hook. His offer to return to her, humbled on his knees (even though he was himself the injured party), had pleased her. He now waited for her to speak. Time was running out. The curfew was only an hour away.

He wondered if she had noticed that he'd started parting his hair on the left side, not in the middle, as before. If only he could also change his name, his profession—everything. He wanted a clean break with the past.

'All right,' Sarita said. 'Let things take their own course.'

As he now rose to leave, he snatched a glance at the canvas hanging just above the mantelpiece—Jamini Roy's impressionistic painting of a beggar girl, staring out of her hollow, sunken eyes—oh, the look of some dark anguish. He'd bought it in Calcutta during one of his professional visits there. How he wished he could ask her for this painting. Silly man, he said to himself, asking for little things when he was gambling for such high stakes.

Hardly had he moved towards the door when Purnima shuffled in, with Rahul in her arms.

'Ma'am, he's been whimpering away in his room. Perhaps it's time for his glass of milk.'

'Surely, you could have given it to him yourself,' Sarita snapped at the servant.

It was surprising, Gautam thought, how she hadn't noticed that the child had slipped away. Was it his offer of remarriage that had absorbed her so completely?

'Take care of yourself,' she said, as he walked to the door. But this time, her voice had mellowed in a genuine concern for his safety.

'Daddy, when will you come back?' Rahul's lisping voice now caught his ears.

'I'll be back soon, my darling,' Gautam replied, and vanished out of the door.

The street lights had been turned on and, in the house opposite, behind a half-drawn curtain, a face hung close to the window. It must be Trivedi, Gautam surmised, as he strode towards the main road.

4

After walking briskly through the bylanes of Darya Ganj, Gautam came to Faiz Bazaar, which looked completely deserted—no taxi or tonga anywhere. Although Neel Kamal was still open, the tobacconist under the peepal tree had pulled down his shutters and was gone for the day. An eerie quiet had fallen on both sides of the main road.

Since time was running out, Gautam decided to walk the entire length of Faiz Bazaar, and up Asaf Ali Road, hoping to find some taxi near the Ajmeri Gate, or further down the bridge overlooking Ram Nagar. He knew that he must somehow reach Anand Parbat (the locality in which he was staying) before the curfew, otherwise he'd be helplessly stranded on the way.

Near the Turkman Gate, one of the strongholds of fanatic Muslims, he was challenged by a young man in a fez. Instead of stopping, Gautam jumped across the pavement onto the other side of Asaf Ali Road, and hid himself behind a tea-stall on the eastern edge of Ramlila Grounds. The man set upon the chase was, however, closing in fast.

Suddenly, a police jeep pulled up alongside the tea-stall, and an officer with a perky moustache asked him in an aggressive Punjabi accent. 'Hiding away? . . . Who are you?'

Gautam emerged from behind the stall, a little shattered and confused. But on seeing a police officer, he felt secure.

'Gautam Mehta, assistant editor of *The Challenge*,' he replied.

'But this is not the time, Mr Mehta, to be out.' The officer's voice was now polite. 'It will soon be curfew time, and we have orders to shoot at sight anyone out on the streets.'

'I'm sorry,' said Gautam. 'I wasn't reporting. I just went to see someone and couldn't find a taxi anywhere.'

'How far are you going?'

'Anand Parbat, beyond Karol Bagh.'

'Maybe I could give you a ride as far as Pahar Ganj.'

'That would be a great help. Thank you very much.'

Hardly had the jeep rattled across the Ajmeri Gate flyover bridge when the officer braked it to a stop. Right ahead, all along Pahar Ganj, a terrible blaze of fire—yellow, brown and red flames—was shooting into the sky. Since Gautam was quite familiar with this street, he surmised that the fire had engulfed all the timber shops in this area—the godowns stacked with teak, bamboo and deodar. The incensed flames were gutting everything in their way.

'I'm sorry, Mr Mehta,' said the police officer, 'I can't take you any further. It looks like I'll be stuck here for a while.' Then he added, after a moment's pause, 'It must be those bloody Muslim arsonists.'

Gautam realized that the officer was a bigoted Hindu.

'Thank you very much for the ride,' Gautam said, and he jumped off the vehicle.

The fire had now engulfed a four-storeyed building looming above one of the timber shops, and frantic screams were coming from the top floor. By now a large crowd had gathered, yelling for revenge. Instead of making way for the fire engines, groups of people stood excitedly around, blocking the road and shouting, 'Har Har Mahadev!'

Gautam heard a man cry out: 'It was a missile from the Ajmeri Mosque that set it off! I saw it myself! Kill those bastard Muslims, those Pakistani spies!'

In spite of the imminent curfew, hordes of people from the neighbouring areas started swarming in. As Gautam decided to pull himself out of this maelstrom, he noticed a few young men passing knives and sticks of explosives all around. So the lines were being drawn up; soon there would be another battle.

The sky was now pitch dark. Since most of the street lights had been smashed during the rioting, Gautam wouldn't have been able to find his way home for the glare of the fire.

Suddenly, a hush descended over the place. Everyone stepped aside to make way for a huge open car, escorted by several jeeps. Then a heavily decorated officer stood up in the car, and blared into a microphone. It was a deep, resonant voice, minatory and merciless, shooting off ultimatums like the yapp-yapp of a Bren gun: 'I give you all just fifteen minutes—no more. Get off the streets and back to your homes. Make your choice—life or death. In a quarter of an hour, I will order my men to start firing.'

'Ah, Thornton sahib, the commissioner of police!' someone whispered.

The word flashed all around like the relentless blaze which was still raging away, despite the firemen's efforts.

As the thunderous voice stopped, a volley of guns boomed into the air. This was a clear signal that Thornton sahib meant business. Now there was no shouting, only mute curses.

'That mongrel of a police commissioner!' someone said. 'Why doesn't he go over to the Turkman Gate and control those bastards?' Another voice joined in: 'These hybrid Englishmen were always for the Muslims!' . . . 'Stupid Nehru—to let our enemies stay on, Mountbatten and Thornton!' 'No, don't say that of Pandit Mountbatten—he's now one of us.'

Gautam was amused to hear these tarty comments. Obviously, none of them had heard of Father Jones, otherwise he too would have come in for some sniping.

Gautam started walking briskly towards the Dayanand Anglo-Vedic Higher Secondary School. The crowd had now begun to thin away and Pahar Ganj looked like a forsaken fortress. By the time he reached home, it was a quarter to ten—just fifteen minutes before the curfew was due to begin.

'You shouldn't have risked staying away so long, Gautam,' said his father, as he answered the door.

'I know, Dad. But I was helplessly caught on the way.'

'Good heavens!' his father exclaimed, tense and worried. 'Come right in. You do look all nerves.'

Gautam felt like a fugitive who is offered shelter. While his mother rushed to the kitchen to fix him some supper, his father kept staring at Gautam. Shamlal wondered how his son had fared during the day.

Weary-footed, Gautam retired to his room and changed into his white kurta and pyjamas. He dropped down on the divan which had been improvised as a settee with a cotton-stuffed mattress, and three long bolsters.

His parents had arrived in Delhi after many harrowing experiences on the way from Lahore. Though they were fatigued and their nerves were frazzled, Gautam couldn't keep them with him for more than a few days. They'd been looking forward to seeing their grandson, but soon they felt unhoused—their second partition, as his mother called it. Sarita had made it impossible for them to stay in the house. She had married an individual, she kept dinning into Gautam's ears, not a family. Then came the shocking revelation about Sarita and the child.

Gautam thought it prudent to let them move into a small house at Anand Parbat. Fortunately, his father had been offered the post of the secretary to the managing committee, Dayanand College, more out of recognition for his past association with the Arya Samaj, Anarkali, Lahore, than for his administrative experience.

In Lahore, Shamlal Mehta had been known for his zeal for the Hindu dharma. He had organized several successful rallies against the British missionaries, who held public discourses against Hinduism and distributed handsomely bound free copies of the Bible. They also tempted many poor Hindus into Christianity by offering them the bait of social security—good jobs, quick out-of-turn promotions . . .

Shamlal Mehta felt like a crusader against the combined

might of the British Empire and the Anglican Church. He held counter-rallies in the city to expose 'the insidious designs' of the rulers. 'It isn't so much their political domination as their subtle, devious assault on our dharma,' he always said in public. 'This may some day undermine our great civilization.' Many times he was warned by the secret police, but this dedicated banner-holder for Swami Dayanand continued to fire away, emboldened by the national movement for independence that had picked up a new momentum in the early 1940s.

Now he had been adequately rewarded by the Delhi Arya Samaj Prabandhak Committee with a sinecure job—and free official accommodation, just when he had been dislodged by his daughter-in-law. An old two-room house, near Karol Bagh, atop an ancient hill called Anand Parbat, was a virtual boon.

It wasn't really a house, only a battered cottage with a tin roof that rattled whenever the hot winds blew across the hill. If it hadn't been a dry month, the rains would have pounded the wobbly, cracked tin sheets, making sleep at night impossible.

The room in the rear had been taken over by Gautam as his temporary lodging. Here he would sit at the steel-barred window, which looked like the porthole of a sinking ship, and look at an open patch of land littered with garbage. There, behind a cluster of grey weather-beaten boulders, the street urchins would sometimes stop to urinate.

The room in front was used by his parents as a bedsitter. On the wall facing their bed hung a faded painting of Swami Dayanand, a knotted stump in one hand, a copy of the *Satyarath Prakash* in the other. He looked like a self-assured wrestler out to twist the arm of anyone who dared to challenge him.

In a corner of the covered verandah, beyond this room, Gautam's mother had improvised her kitchen—a small wooden cupboard for utensils and crockery, hastily salvaged from their house in Lahore. It was also used as a bathroom. Immediately after the morning tea, a curtain was pulled down to ensure privacy. As for the lavatory, everybody had to queue up in the morning, in front of a shed that served about half a dozen families of the teaching and administrative staff of the Dayanand College. In fact, this part of Anand Parbat looked like one of those refugee colonies that had sprung up all over Delhi—from Kingsway Camp to the Lodi Estate. Gautam, however, felt much happier here with his parents, in spite of the grimy environs.

Patiently, Gautam's parents let him have his food; then Shamlal said in a gentle voice: 'It must have been a terrible day for you.'

'Yes, Dad.'

'How did it go with the bishop?' Shamlal couldn't bridle his curiosity any longer.

'It's all arranged. I've been asked to bring along a witness next Thursday . . . It should take only a few minutes.'

Gautam sounded as though he had to undergo a surgical operation, brief but assuredly successful.

His father felt a little piqued at his son's niggardly response. He wanted to hear the entire story, every detail. He also wanted to know if Gautam had seen 'that woman'—Sarita's name was no longer mentioned in the house.

'Would you like me to come along?' asked his father.

'Relatives, as you know, are never recognized as witnesses.'

Outside, a man stopped beside a rock to urinate, but hearing voices across the window, buttoned up and slunk away. By now his mother, who'd been listening to them from the kitchen, also came in. She took a seat quietly in a corner, near the window.

'Then I'll stay away,' said Shamlal. 'But who'll be your witness?'

'Berry.'

'I should have guessed.'

Gautam's father now assumed a sombre expression; his brow darkened as he looked blankly out of the window. Gautam wondered if he was under some strain. Had he really reconciled himself to his son's conversion? Had he really forsaken his infallible prophet, Maharishi Dayanand, whom he ranked above the Buddha, Guru Nanak and Gandhi—even above Lord Krishna?

Gautam snatched another glance at his father, who sat there glum and anxious, his forehead wrinkled, his chiselled chin drooping. Was it a gnawing awareness of some nemesis overtaking him? Or, because Jesus was about to claim his only child by offering him the bait, not of social security but of easy divorce.

'Is there anything bothering you, Dad?'

'No, nothing whatsoever,' he replied. But his voice came loaded with poignancy: 'You know, Gautam,' he resumed, 'I've done some hard thinking during the past few days . . . Maybe Christ too was a yogi, a real karma yogi.'

He nodded his head as if to underscore his words.

Ah, the recantation! Gautam at once realized that he

was listening to an indulgent father who'd surrendered his soul to the devil. Indeed, there came in the life of everyone a moment when one would seek any desperate justification for one's lapses.

Gautam merely smiled.

'I know you are amused,' Shamlal said. 'But I do mean it, really. Well, if the Resurrection is an absurd fantasy according to the Hindus, how do you explain the equally inconceivable phenomenon of our yogis burying themselves underground for days together, then emerging with their heartbeats normal, their vision clear as crystal?'

'But Christ died on the cross, nailed and bleeding till the end. Stone-dead he was when they pulled him down.'

'No, my dear, Christ didn't die on the cross,' said Shamlal. 'He was left there unconscious by the Romans as 'stone-dead' and buried later. But now I earnestly believe that being a yogi, he had controlled his organs, had sort of anaesthetized himself before they nailed him on the cross. And since he went into a deep Samadhi, a yogic trance, he felt no pain—nor did he really die, so, he rose from his grave after a brief spell of what I think was a kind of subterranean meditation. That was the Resurrection!'

'It appears I've lost you both to Jesus Christ.'

It was Gautam's mother who interjected in a mocking tone. She was intrigued by her husband's ingenious interpretation of Christ's rebirth. She'd always admired his brilliance, his unrivalled supremacy in polemics, but wasn't he now arguing like the devil himself? It was indeed a great relief for her to know that her son would soon get his divorce. But beyond that point, she thought, all such talk was blatant hypocrisy.

Mrs Radha Mehta's Hindu orthodoxy could never let her accept the notion of Jesus Christ as a yogi. She'd already decided to bring her son back to Hinduism after the divorce was settled. She would let her son stay with Jesus for only a year, the safe period, as counselled by his lawyer. In fact, she was excited at the prospect of looking around for a suitable bride for her son—someone who would be truly devoted to him.

So, rather bored by this theological dialectic between father and son, she gently reminded them of the important broadcasts that evening by Lord Louis Mountbatten and Jawaharlal Nehru. Without waiting for the father and son to stop, she moved into the other room to turn on the radio.

First came the well-known announcer, Melville de Mellow: 'Please stand by for an important broadcast by His Excellency, Lord Louis Mountbatten, the Governor-General of India.'

A moment's pause, in which one could hear the faint rustling of papers. Then came on a voice—suave, deep and commanding—with each word rolling out in a clipped British accent.

Mountbatten started off with his homage to the great Indian heritage, particularly its religious tradition of tolerance and forgiveness. Then he exhorted the new India to live up to these lofty values: let all communities live in peace and enjoy the fruits of freedom. Discreetly avoiding any reference to Pakistan, he urged all Indians to now arm themselves for a much tougher battle—for peace and prosperity. Finally, he thanked India for the respect and affection she had shown him—which symbolized the new bond of friendship between India and England.

This speech, with its poised rhetoric and staid urbanity, impressed Shamlal Mehta. In another frame of mind, he would have sensed some insidious motive—a member of the royalty trying to perpetuate the Empire through the subtlest form of diplomacy. And wouldn't the oblique operation of proselytization derive sustenance from the chief executive of free India—a Christian?

But, sitting there, facing Gautam and his mother, he said: 'The best of Englishmen! Surely Nehru or Patel couldn't have run the country's administration on their own. Agitational politics is one thing but the capacity to rule quite another.'

Gautam, however, said nothing. He merely tried to anticipate his own paper's reaction to this speech.

The voice that next took the air was Nehru's. He started with a sharp thrust: 'This is not the freedom we'd fought for—this is not the India of Mahatma Gandhi's dreams! When will the Hindus realize that this country is not theirs alone? Can we forget the great sacrifices made by such national leaders as Maulana Abul Kalam Azad and Khan Abdul Ghaffar Khan? The Father of the Nation is at present in Noakhali, nursing the wounds of our Muslim brethren. But here, in this historic capital of India, this city of ancient splendour, we're indulging in senseless violence.

'Let there be no ill will against Pakistan; we wish that country peace and prosperity. But if our frontiers are threatened, we shall fight to the last. So let's not waste our energies in mutual destruction. We have hitched our destiny to the stars; we have miles to go and promises to keep. Let's march together, hand in hand—resolute, unflinching and fearless—till we mould the India of our dreams. Jai Hind!'

'That's our young prince—a sort of Hamlet,' said Shamlal. 'Cambridge-educated like Mountbatten, but too flamboyant, too poetic, too impractical. I hope he'll learn to run the administration.'

Gautam's mother beamed at her husband's somersault. Turning towards her son, she said: 'Isn't your father completely sold out to the British? Next time he may argue that Jesus was not Jewish but English!'

'That's a naïve woman,' said Shamlal. But his eyes glistened as they rested fondly on her face. 'How can you make her understand anything?' Then to Gautam: 'You must be terribly tired. Why don't you go to bed? I'll settle up with your mother in my own way.'

But before his father moved off to his bedroom, Gautam looked at his face closely. Such a striking resemblance with Abdul Rahim—the same arched eyebrows, the same chiselled chin and nose.

'Oh, the dead man's letter!' Gautam suddenly recalled.

He reached out for his jacket, hanging on a peg above the divan, and fumbled for the letter in its inner pocket. Yes, there it was. Smoothing out the blood-stained paper, his eyes caught the last words: 'Sometimes I wonder why our British rulers chose to leave us to these Hindu bloodsuckers.'

How very ironic, Gautam said to himself, that both communities were still looking to England for help.

He put away the letter, muttering to himself: 'Tomorrow, I'll write to his wife.'

Lying in bed, he began to compose the letter mentally. How should I break the news? Who was Salma? Haseena's sister, presumably. And where exactly was Haseena in

Delhi? He conjured up the image of an abducted Muslim girl, held under duress somewhere in the capital. Supposing *he* had a sister kidnapped and carried away to Pakistan! He also thought of the Sikh driver's two sisters . . . He jerked his head as though to shake off these gruesome images. Thank God, he didn't have a sister.

In the other room, the light had been turned off. And then the sound of a creaking bed, a fervent kiss, mute whispering.

'Don't be silly—not tonight . . .' That was his mother's voice.

'Why not?'

'Can't you see he's still awake?'

'I'll wait.'

'I said, not tonight.'

'I thought you'd also like to celebrate. Isn't Gautam getting his divorce?'

His father pressed on, his voice throbbing with passion.

'You know once I say no—that's it,' his mother replied. 'And I'm not really in the mood. Not after your impassioned rechristening of Jesus as a Hindu yogi . . . Maybe next Thursday.'

'Oh God, what a tyrant!'

But a few minutes later, Gautam again heard the bed creaking. This time there were no words spoken, only muffled breathing, deep and intense.

So his father had had his way after all, Gautam understood.

Old lovers! Of course, even at fifty-nine his father was sinewy and full-blooded. For hadn't Gautam's mother fed him daily on creamed milk, almonds and Chavanprash?

And she had herself, at fifty-three, never forsaken her nail polish. And daily she rubbed her cheeks with orange peels to lend them a fresh glow.

Lying in bed, as Gautam peered out of the window, he saw the moon sailing into a forest of clouds, like a lonely traveller. Under its silvery shine, the boulders looked like primordial mammals resting on their broad haunches, grinding their jaws.

5

'Is he there?' Gautam asked, as Shyama, Berry's maidservant, answered the door.

'Yes, sir,' she replied, 'but still in bed.'

'Well past ten, and still sleeping?' he said, walking straight over to Berry's bedroom.

'He kept working late last night,' Shyama said, as she followed him demurely.

'And Memsahib—is she up?'

'She didn't return last night. She'd gone to see her ailing aunt and stayed back there,' Shyama chattered on, 'because of the curfew . . . We had a big fire in Pahar Ganj . . .'

'Yes, I know.'

Berry, Gautam thought, must have had a free night, with Sonali away and Shyama alone in the house—and much too willing.

He again glanced at this woman and noticed that she was wearing one of Sonali's Kanchivaram saris, and through the translucent blouse were visible two ripe breasts, unencumbered with any brassiere. Her long hair tumbled over her shoulders, down to her swaying hips. Her cheeks rouged, a large moon-shaped kumkum on her forehead, she walked about with a tantalizing swish.

'Would you care for some coffee, sir?' she asked, a proprietary ring in her voice as though, till Sonali's return, she was mistress of the house.

'Later,' Gautam said, as he knocked at Berry's bedroom. 'Let me first shake this lazy thing out of his dreams.'

'Is it you, Shyama?' came Berry's languorous voice.

'It's Mehta sahib, sir.'

That was very discreetly done, this 'stirring' up of her master, Gautam thought. He turned the doorknob and walked in.

'You indolent thing, dreaming away so late.'

'Hello, Gautam,' Berry said drowsily, as he gathered himself up in bed and threw his massive body against a couple of large, feathery pillows. 'That's a nice surprise. Couldn't get any sleep last night—a terrible fire in the neighbourhood and the beastly shouting . . .'

'Or was it the play in bed?' Gautam jibed, whispering. 'Working away late in the night? How very ingenious of you to send Sonali away . . .'

'Take it easy, Gautam,' he smiled, rolling his tongue over his lips, leeringly.

'Smooth operator! One of these days, I'm going to tell Sonali everything.'

'But dare she complain?' Berry asked, his hairy chest, like that of a large ape, emerging from under the covers, his hand reaching out for a cigar on the side-table. 'She knows,' he added, 'that if she creates a scene, out she goes. A wife should be broken into complete submission from the very beginning, otherwise she can give you hell.'

'You sound like a lion tamer.'

'Or would you rather have me end up a sulking, suffering cuckold—like yourself?'

As Gautam winced, Berry realized that he'd hurt his friend.

'I didn't mean to . . .' he said, now caressing Gautam's hand. 'In a sense, we are both kindred souls. If you've been the victim of adultery, my wife has killed me with her unalloyed devotion. That stumpy, insipid creature! So you see, we are both fellow-sufferers.'

But even this facetiousness didn't take the edge off his previous barb.

Yes, Gautam thought, it was all his own fault, his over trustfulness, his utter spinelessness. How Berry had always fought back in life, tenaciously, valorously. Even now his chief engineer was hell-bent on suspending him on some trumped-up charge, just because Berry wouldn't cringe before him. What if he couldn't move up the professional ladder? Wasn't he willing to retire as a mere assistant mechanical engineer?

'You know, Berry, I almost came over to see you last evening, but now I realize that would have been a rude intrusion.'

'Not at all,' he said. 'Shyama could have waited in the wings for a while . . . A friend always comes first. I never mix up my priorities.'

The servant came in with two coffees on a silver tray. 'Look, how well she takes care of me,' said Berry.

The woman blushed, threw the flap of her sari over her breasts and withdrew briskly from the room.

'That was Sonali's sari, wasn't it?' Gautam asked.

'Yes. But why shouldn't she wear it when the mistress is away?'

'You are a rascal.'

'Maybe—but a benign one.'

Then after a moment's silence, Berry said: 'Well, you haven't come to the point. How did it go at St. John's? Weren't you supposed to meet the bishop yesterday?'

'That was what I came to tell you—something I'll be saying for the third time: first to Sarita, then to my father, and now to you . . . I guess I have hooked the old priest—that gullible Englishman.'

'Bravo!'

'But the real fun is that the man also thinks he has hauled in a big salmon. He deserves to be honoured with a title on the new year—an MBE at least, if not an OBE!'

'I bet he hasn't been here long enough to plumb the Oriental mind—so devious, so scheming, so ruthless.'

Gautam now narrated in detail his encounter with the bishop, and the incident relating to Abdul Rahim.

'I wonder where Haseena is in Delhi,' was Berry's first response. 'I should like to rescue her from her abductors.' There was a lustful glint in his eyes.

'You're an unmitigated lecher,' Gautam said smiling, sensing his intention. 'Your entire life revolves around one axis—woman.'

'But what greater pleasure is there than to hold a woman's breasts in your palms? Then to descend into that deep, dark cavern where eternal peace resides . . . The rest is all maya, mere illusion.'

'Oh, your irrepressible eroticism!'

'Call it whatever you like,' said Berry. 'It keeps you from sulking—and sane and healthy.' Then, after a moment's pause: 'You know I made love to Shyama last night while the timber shops were blazing away in the neighbourhood. Oh God, this woman certainly knows how to swing.'

'Another Nero! That's what you are. But no more of this.' Gautam paused. 'I need your help. Will you come to St. John's next Thursday as my witness?'

'As your bottle-holder?'

'Yes.'

'Any time, anywhere.'

'Thank you . . . Then ten o' clock—at the church.'

'But look, if that woman chooses to back out at the last moment, there'll still be another way out,' Berry said.

'What?'

'Islam. It offers you four wives—that woman plus three.'

'But that won't do. I'll still have that albatross around my neck.'

'She'll then be just one of four.'

'You're in high spirits today,' said Gautam; then, looking at his watch, 'I must get moving now. It's almost eleven.'

But as he was about to leave, Shyama breezed in.

'It's Purnima, sir. She wants to see sahib at once.'

'Purnima!' Gautam exclaimed, almost blanching with anxiety. 'Oh Jesus, what's up now? What if that woman has already changed her mind?'

Quickly Berry changed into his dressing gown, and sat on a sofa chair.

As Purnima appeared at the door, looking pale and worn out, Gautam erupted.

'What's the matter? . . . How did you know I was here?'

'Sir, I first went to Anand Parbat and was told . . .'

'Okay,' said Gautam sharply. 'Will you spit it out? Chasing me round the world like a detective.'

'Rahul's dead, sir!'

'What!' both Gautam and Berry exclaimed, in great surprise.

'Died last night, about three o'clock. Sudden haemorrhage or something.'

A sombre hush fell over the place. Gautam's face went livid; he kept staring at Purnima, as though finding it difficult to believe what he'd just heard. He'd loved the child dearly, spending hours with him in the nursery—brought him toys, candies. And now he was gone.

'But I saw him only last evening, you know,' Gautam said, biting his lips. 'Is the body still there?'

'Yes, sir,' she answered. 'Memsahib thought you might like to see him before he was taken away.'

'Is there nobody else around?' Gautam asked her, suddenly realizing that the other man might also be there.

'Nobody else will be there, sir, till noon.'

Gautam knew that the woman was only being discreet. 'Nobody' was obviously Mohinder. He understood that after his earnest offer of remarriage, Sarita must have felt impelled to make this gesture.

Then came the child's last words ringing into his ears: 'Daddy, when will you come back again?'

'I'll be there, Purnima.'

6

On his way to Darya Ganj, Gautam dropped into a wayside mailbox the letter he'd written to Abdul Rahim's wife. He felt as though he'd been caught between two deaths—the old man's and Rahul's. Wasn't he poised precariously, like a spider, between two ends of a cobweb? A burnt-out young man around thirty! Could he again pick up the threads of his life at this late stage? He knew he was becoming a manic-depressive. He should heed the tonic advice of that daredevil, Berry, he told himself, and grab his share of happiness.

As he approached the house, his mind swung back to Rahul. Why didn't he hate him, this painful remembrance of his wife's infidelity? But that was beyond him, he knew. Even amidst the din of traffic, en route to Darya Ganj, he imagined himself hearing the child's last words.

'Yes, I'm coming to you, my dear,' he said to himself, as he knocked at the door. He hadn't realized that it was already a little after twelve.

Purnima,who'd somehow reached the house ahead of him, answered the door. Quickly, he walked through the drawing room, looking momentarily at Jamini Roy's

'Beggar Girl' with her agonized blank stare. He turned into the bedroom where, on a leather sofa near the double bed, lay Rahul, dressed in the sailor's uniform he'd brought him from Bombay. The child looked as though he was just asleep, tranquil and happy, after the day's hectic play.

All around the sofa ran little rills of water dripping from the large slabs of ice, heaped one on top of the other. Petals of roses and jasmine lay strewn on the sofa, and all over the floor. Since Gautam had removed his shoes out of respect for the dead, he felt the viscid wetness under his bare feet.

As his eyes lingered on Rahul's face, he remained oblivious of Sarita's presence in the room. Sitting on a stool, far away in a corner, she watched him deeply engrossed in the child. Indeed, Gautam loved him very much—his wan face bore ample testimony to it.

Then, as Gautam looked into the corner, their eyes met: a cold, silent encounter, neither of them uttering a word. This woman whose raucous, nagging voice had always rocked the house, now sat mute, almost vanquished. A riffle of compassion ran through him.

Gautam now sat on the sofa, near Rahul, caressed his face and head. But just as he bent to kiss him on the forehead, he heard a knock at the door. Purnima rushed to answer it, but the person had already walked in. Mohinder! Two pairs of glazed eyes collided with each other.

Gautam looked at his watch; it showed a half past twelve. Well, wasn't he himself to blame for first coming late and then overstaying? Hadn't Purnima discreetly assured him that there would be 'nobody' around 'till noon'? Now that he'd stayed on well beyond the deadline, 'Mr Nobody' had made his appearance on the scene—as

Rahul's father and Sarita's paramour. Gautam felt a stab of revulsion for this man and that woman.

Immediately, he got up from the sofa and turned towards the door. He must clear out at once, he thought, and let the real parents take over. Wasn't he like a neighbour who, after offering his condolences, should promptly withdraw? As the three of them looked at one another, it appeared as though they were acting in a pantomime—two men, a woman and a sleeping child.

Then Gautam swung out of the room. Once out of the house, he felt the hot sun beating down his neck. The afternoon heat was sizzling like a furnace. How cool it had been in there, he recalled, near those slabs of ice. But then the other blaze now overtook him—of intense loathing.

He had hardly gone a few yards down the street when he saw Mohinder running after him, breathlessly.

'A moment, p-l-e-a-s-e!'

The words blared into the air; the silence of the past half hour was shattered. What was this man up to? Gautam braced himself for the confrontation.

To hell with this man, he thought; if only he could bash his head against some lamp post.

'I've been wanting to have a word with you, alone.'

'Will you drop the prologue?' Gautam shot off. 'What do you want?'

'I know I've wronged you but, really, I'm not to blame.'

There was strange pathos in his voice. He'd stopped in the middle of the street, his right hand nervously fidgeting with a curl near his forehead.

'I have no time to listen to all this. What's done is done.'

Then, after a pause, he resumed, almost hissing: 'Why don't you marry her now?'

'What do you mean?'

'Surely you understand, you deadly viper,' Gautam blared out.

'Maybe I deserve to be called that . . . But you loved him.'

'Who?'

In his anger, Gautam couldn't fathom what Mohinder had meant.

'Rahul.'

'I don't know,' Gautam almost stuttered and strode away.

A man from the house opposite peeped out. From the street's bend, Gautam looked back to see Trivedi talking to Mohinder.

7

Designed as an inverted charpoy, almost like the King's Chapel at Cambridge, and built three years after the Indian Mutiny, in 1860, St. John's Cathedral stands at the northern end of Mahavir Street, about half a mile from the Red Fort. Its steeples tower high above a marketplace cluttered with hardware merchants, drapers and wholesale dealers in stationery. Except for two painted glass windows on either side of the main entrance, depicting scenes from the Bible, all other windows are bare.

But what strikes even a casual visitor to St. John's is its sturdy massiveness, its impregnable strength. After the end of the British rule, on 15 August 1947, this cathedral acquired a unique significance, as though the Englishman, who first landed on the Indian soil as a mere trader, and later ruled as the absolute monarch of this subcontinent, had now assumed his new role as a missionary. So, all the affluent Anglican missions in England started pouring generous donations into this church which, they believed, was now destined to 'annex' India's spirit, if not her body. No wonder, Father Jones felt himself unequal to the new burdens and responsibilities; so much had happened within the brief span of a few weeks only.

On a quiet warm Thursday morning, Father Jones walked across the vast courtyard, holding a pocket Bible in his right hand. He was draped in a white silken robe, his velvet hood dangling at the nape of his neck. At the main entrance, he was joined by two of his junior churchmen, while inside the cathedral were Gautam and Berry, already seated, looking like two nervous candidates about to be interviewed for some post.

As Father Jones saw Gautam, he walked towards him.

'Good morning Mr Mehta,' he greeted him with a gracious smile.

'Good morning, Father,' Gautam responded; then, turning to Berry, he added, 'This is my friend, Birendra Dhawan. He'll be my witness.'

'I'm very pleased to meet you, Mr Dhawan . . .'

Then the bishop beckoned Gautam to follow him up the rostrum. To its left stood a large bronze statue of Christ on the Cross, while to the right was a mural painting of the Madonna and the Child. As Gautam went down on his knees, Father Jones began to read from the Bible. Gautam was particularly touched by a passage from Joshua in which Moses asks his followers to cross the river Jordan into the land of new promise. Wasn't he too about to cross over to freedom!

This was followed by the sprinkling of holy water on his head and shoulders. As Gautam rose to his feet, the bishop said: 'Since you are now one of Jesus's flock, the Lord shall take care of you.'

There was a brief silence. Then the bishop asked the small congregation to join him in prayer.

'O Lord, this man has come to you for your blessing. Let him share your glory, partake of your divine grace. All these years he has wandered about seeking you, and now that he kneels at your feet, accept him, O Lord—help him, guide him, forgive him all his past sins. He seems to have suffered endlessly. What joy can there be without you? So for every moment of pain he has undergone, let him have years of happiness. Lend him courage, for that's what he'll need most hereafter. Fill the remaining years of his life with love, light and song. Amen!'

After this simple ceremony, Father Jones led everyone into his office in the rear wing of the cathedral, where Gautam signed in a large brown register. Berry put his signature as his witness. The other two churchmen signed on behalf of St. John's Association. Immediately thereafter, Gautam received a large golden card, which looked like a wedding invitation.

After shaking hands with the bishop and thanking him profusely, Gautam and Berry hurried across the churchyard to the front gate. Here Gautam showed him the spot where he'd seen Abdul Rahim's body lying in a pool of blood.

Hardly had they stepped out of the cathedral when Berry turned on his banter: 'How do you feel, Mr Moses Kaufmann?'

'I'm not Jewish, I'm Christian,' Gautam replied, smiling.

'Not that I'd know the difference . . . Still, do you feel any different?'

'Not quite,' Gautam answered, solemnly this time. 'But how did the bishop's prayer strike you? . . . Wishing me years of happiness and all that. If only he knew how much I needed such a blessing. Of course, pain for Father Jones is merely living without Christ, not the trauma of a wife's betrayal.'

'Religion never gets that far anyway,' said Berry. 'But the prayer was certainly very moving, even for someone like me. These people, however, are quite professional, you know,' he continued. 'They know how to spout such mouthfuls.'

'Oh, you unbelieving thing!' Gautam said, nudging him. 'You don't know what you're missing. How would your Hindu priest have done it? He would have just chanted a few Sanskrit mantras, asked you to sit cross-legged near the sacred fire, and thrown spoonfuls of ghee and camphor into the flames . . . These pundits are real ringmasters, you know, mumbling incomprehensibly all the time.'

'Bravo!' Berry exclaimed. 'Already gone overboard! You'll make a blooming fanatic Christian, surely.'

'I don't know,' said Gautam. 'But you can't deny that Jesus has been my real saviour.'

'Here's then an occasion for celebration,' Berry said. 'Even a hot cup of tea should do since the bars wouldn't serve whisky at this time . . . I wonder, though, what's wrong with drinking whisky at noon? Stupid conventions!'

'I know if you had a pool of Scotch in your house, you'd be swimming about like a Chinese goldfish, from dawn to dusk, till you'd boozed it all off.'

'What a thought! I wish I had the money to do it, really.'

As they stopped by a wayside tea-stall, further down Mahavir Street, an outburst of shouting hit their ears—'Allah-ho-Akbar!' There appeared from the street's bend a large mob of Muslims armed with knives, swords, spears and sticks. The crowd was led by a young tough who was blaring away through a microphone: 'Khoon ka badla khoon! Blood for blood!' The others joined in: 'Kill the bloody kafirs! Castrate them! Rape their women!' It was all rounded off with a piercing yell: 'Ya Ali, ya Mohammad!'

The tea vendor, a Hindu, at once pulled down his shutters and disappeared into the house behind his stall, leaving Gautam and Berry alone on the pavement. Before they could flee, a middle-aged man from the crowd had already spotted them.

'There—catch those kafirs!' he bawled.

Instantly, three hoodlums, brandishing their knives and swords, closed in. The first, a moustached fellow, caught Gautam by the collar and nearly lifted him off the ground like a sack of rice, while the other two pounced upon Berry.

'Spare us please—we're Christians!' Berry pleaded.

The moustached creature now dropped Gautam and turned to Berry.

'We'll find out if you're lying.'

A fourth man who'd joined the others shouted: 'Strip them!'

But before they could do anything, Berry called out to Gautam: 'Show them the card, brother', then, looking at the assailants, he said, 'or, you may ask Father Jones at St. John's, just across the street.'

'All right,' said a bystander, holding a long spear in his left hand. 'Let's see the card.'

At once Gautam pulled out his certificate of conversion and handed it to the moustached fellow, who appeared to be utterly illiterate. Turning it over in his hand, he looked blankly at the words.

'Let's go—they're Christians all right,' he said.

The mob hustled onward, leaving Gautam and Berry dazed and unnerved. They knew that if they tried to bolt they'd again arouse suspicion. No, they should walk away casually into some bylane.

Suddenly a side-door on the pavement opened and a hand pulled Berry inside.

'Ask your friend in too,' said the man, in a whisper.

'But we're Christians,' Berry mumbled, his face losing colour.

'Never mind,' came the prompt reply. 'I've heard it all through my window. I'm only trying to help you both.'

'Thank you, but . . .'

Berry's eyes fell on a wall calendar showing a massive-chested Swami Dayanand, a stump in one hand and the *Satyarath Prakash* in the other. 'Ah, an Arya Samajist!' he said to himself, in a spurt of recognition.

At once Berry stepped out and pushed Gautam inside, who was looking about stupefied.

'It's all right,' whispered Berry.

But Gautam too had seen the calendar.

'Is your friend really a Christian?' the man asked Berry.

'Well, sort of . . .'

'What do you mean?'

'That's a long story,' said Berry.

'Oh, you don't want to tell me. But then neither of you looks Christian. It's just my instinct!' the man said, with a sparkle of omniscience in his eyes. He then turned to Berry. 'And is he your brother?'

'A friend. And I'm a Hindu—sort of.'

'Quite amusing,' the man said. 'Two sorts!' After a brief pause, somewhat puzzled, he asked, 'Your names, please?'

'I'm Birender Dhawan,' Berry replied, 'and he's Gautam Mehta.'

'That has cleared up a lot of mystery.' The man smiled.

'Has it?' Berry would have laughed out but for the gruesomeness of the situation.

'Well, I'm Gopinath Trivedi and, since we're just a few Hindu families around here, I always put up a large green flag with a crescent, whenever a Muslim mob passes by.'

'Very ingenious,' said Gautam, who had so far kept silent.

Gopinath felt somewhat exposed before these young men. Was he, after all, any different from them? But in these turbulent times, announcing one's identity on any occasion could be sheer foolhardiness. Perhaps, he thought, even Swami Dayanand would have condoned such a subterfuge.

Gopinath now ushered them into his drawing room. 'You may have to wait here awhile,' he said, 'The mob is still prowling about. They're out to avenge the killing, a few days ago, of an old Muslim, near St. John's.'

'Yes, I know,' Gautam said.

'Heard about it?'

'I was there when it happened.'

'Do you live around here?'

'No, I live,' then suddenly Gautam realized that he should have said *he used to live until a few days ago*, 'in Darya Ganj, down Geeta Street.'

Gopinath's face brightened up.

'Interesting,' he said. 'I have a cousin who lives out there—Padamnath Trivedi.'

'Of course, I know him very well,' said Gautam. 'He's my neighbour.'

'Is he? God help you,' he said. 'Well, I'm a little scared of him—he's too meddlesome.'

'Then you should know him better,' Gautam said, thinking it unwise to speak out about this scandalmonger.

Since Gautam didn't hear any other voice in the house, he wondered if this man lived alone, like his cousin. But he certainly sounded quite different, so gracious and helpful.

There was a brief silence. While Berry and Gautam sat near the window, Gopinath took a seat in a corner, under the mantelpiece. Suddenly, there was another outburst of yelling in the street. As Berry drew aside the curtain, he exclaimed: 'Oh God!' and looked away. Then Gautam and Gopinath also peered through, only to look stunned.

An old shaggy cow, that was muzzling into a heap of garbage for something to chew, had been hemmed in by a few Muslims.

'The kafir cow!' one of them shouted, and hurled his spear at the animal.

The weapon pierced through its emaciated belly, letting out a jet of deep, red blood. It was amazing to see how even this skeletal animal had hoarded up so much blood. The cow bellowed out in pain, almost a heart-rending human cry, then slumped to the ground, bashing its head against a lamp post.

The others now swooped down upon it with knives and spears, tearing apart its body, limb by limb. On their faces, glowing with demoniac rage in the blazing summer sun, was the lust for blood—the blood of even a 'Hindu cow'. As the animal lay still in its pool of blood, a vulture flapped down from a nearby tree and began to tear apart its intestines.

The sight nauseated Gautam so much that he nearly threw up.

'What satanic butchery!' he said. 'Strange, how even the animals have been branded Hindu.'

'Is it the aggrieved heart of a Hindu?' asked Gopinath.

'No,' replied Gautam. 'It has nothing to do with my being a Hindu or a Christian. The sight of any killing, of man or animal, sickens me.'

'Even the killing of a pig?'

'Of course.'

'Are you sure?' Gopinath asked, smiling.

Gautam was too deeply agitated to let this man turn on his banter amidst such a grim spectacle. He stood up and asked Berry: 'Shouldn't we be moving on?'

'It seems the cow has done it for you,' Gopinath pressed on. 'But you know you can't leave—the coast is not yet clear.'

'It looks all right now,' Gautam said, looking through the curtain. 'Only a few stragglers out there—all unarmed, I guess. The fury has spent itself out.' Then rising, he said to Berry, 'Come, let's go.'

But Gopinath, who was now afraid of remaining alone in the house, again tried to dissuade them: 'I think it's only a lull before the next storm,' he said. 'It may erupt any time.'

'Not so soon,' said Berry. 'Both parties will need a little time for the next round. So this is the moment to sneak out.'

But hardly had they moved to the front door when they heard a poignant cry—a woman's. Rushing back to the window, they looked through the curtains again and saw a few assaulters pulling away at a young woman's sari, while a man in dhoti and kurta stood close by with folded hands, beseeching them to let her go. Suddenly, one of the ruffians turned around to kick him in the stomach.

'How stupidly mistaken I was to take those stragglers for innocuous pedestrians,' said Gautam.

Dumbfounded, they all kept peering through the curtains, witnessing the gruesome spectacle near the rear end of the tea-stall, just a few feet away.

'A real catch!' said the tallest of the assaulters, who seemed to be their leader.

'Let's carry her away,' said another.

The man in dhoti drew near, and cried out: 'Spare her, please—she's my sister.'

'Good for her,' grinned the leader. 'We'll let you have her first so that she knows the difference between a grass-eater and a beef-eater.

The words lanced through Gautam's heart. 'What wanton lechery!' he muttered.

'Oh please, be merciful,' the woman's brother again implored. 'We were on our way to see our sick mother.'

'Then we'll have your mother too. We'll ravish the whole lot of you—bloody grass-eaters!'

The man now began to tear away at the woman's sari, which came off, then the petticoat, the blouse, the bra, till she stood totally stripped, trying in vain to cover up her breasts with her hands.

As her brother again struggled to intervene, a hefty

fellow whipped out his knife and stabbed him in the back. Then he threatened to plunge it into his heart.

'Don't kill my brother, please,' the woman entreated, her lips trembling. 'Oh Lord, save my brother!' she shrieked.

But the cry whizzed idly past their ears. The leader had already pushed her against the wall, and was now pulling at her breasts.

'All right, let her brother live,' he suddenly told the hefty creature who had threatened to kill him. 'Maybe, she'll then cooperate,' he laughed. 'Isn't that a deal, honey?'

'Kill me instead!' the woman sobbed.

'That wouldn't help, my love. We've so much to do. Where can I find such taut breats, such fragile lips?'

With a lascivious sparkle in his eyes, his mouth went for her breasts.

Gautam could take it no longer. Blood shot into his eyes, and his temples began to throb.

'Can't we do something, Berry? Must we stand here impotently?'

'It isn't that we are impotent, Gautam—this just isn't our moment. It would be certain death if we tried to save them now. It's very agonizing, I know, but . . .'

'He's right,' said Gopinath.

'So we just sit here and watch the show?' Gautam asked, his entire body shaking like a leaf.

'Let's move away from the window,' said Berry.

For the first time Berry realized that such a public exposure of nudity could kill all sexual urge in a man. Ordinarily, he would have felt aroused to see a young woman stripped. But now he felt as though he'd himself been abused and humiliated.

What distressed Berry most was his utter helplessness. He had always been proud of his physique. If the assaulters had been unarmed, he would have certainly charged into them like a wild bull. He'd have wrenched the neck of their leader, even if subsequently he would have been overpowered by the others.

Suddenly, the sound of a shrill siren hit their ears.

'It's the police van,' Berry shouted excitedly, as he opened the window. 'Thank God, they've arrived—at least once, at the right moment.'

At the sight of the police, the entire gang bolted from the scene, carrying away the woman's clothes. Seizing a large tablecloth from the dining room Berry rushed out.

'Wrap yourself in this, please,' Berry said to the woman, giving her the tablecloth. Then he hurried forward, signalling the van to stop. A swarthy young officer jumped off, and almost grunted.

'What's it, man?'

'A bunch of Muslim goons tried to rape a Hindu woman,' Berry said, breathlessly.

'Where are they?' the officer asked, rather nonchalantly.

'They've vanished into some bylane.'

'And what were you doing all this time? Watching the fun?' the officer taunted.

'They were armed,' Gautam intervented, walking up to the van.

'And are you both eunuchs? Couldn't you have picked up something—a stick or a crowbar? Always waiting for the police to come to your rescue.'

Although there was some truth in the officer's barb, his cockiness stung Gautam. As he looked closely at his face, he noticed a white patch of leucoderma on his left cheek, and a deep cut on his chin. He wondered if the officer's ugliness was responsible for his uppishness.

'And what are the police officers supposed to do?' Gautam flashed out. 'Go careering about in their vans?'

'Shut up!' the officer barked. 'Telling us what to do? Who are you, anyway?'

'Gautam Mehta, assistant editor of *The Challenge*,' Gautam snapped back. 'And may I have your name, please? . . . Perhaps I should report to Thornton sahib . . .'

At the mention of the police commissioner's name, the officer went pale.

'I'm sorry, sir,' he mumbled, sheepishly. 'We're trying to do our best.'

'Are you?' Gautam quipped. 'Always arriving a little too late, and then shouting away at everyone.'

'I apologize.'

But Gautam pressed on: 'This place has been through hell during the past two hours: a cow slaughtered, a woman nearly raped, her brother stabbed. And no sign of the police anywhere around.' Then, pointing to the woman who'd by now wrapped herself in the tablecloth, and to her brother who stood drenched in blood, he added: 'There, look at them!'

'I'll personally escort the lady to her house and arrange for immediate medical aid for her brother,' said the officer.

'That would be very nice of you, indeed,' Gautam said, now mellowed.

Both Gautam and Berry waited till the woman and her brother were helped into the van by the officer's aides. As the vehicle snorted into motion, the woman's eyes turned towards Gautam and Berry—a pair of eyes, deep and moist. Her lips quivered as though she wanted to say something. But it was her brother who spoke: 'I don't know how to thank you both.'

'That's all right,' said Gautam. 'I hope the wound isn't too deep.'

'No, sir . . . I'll be okay.'

As the van zoomed away, Gautam turned to Gopinath.

'And how shall we thank you, Mr Trivedi?'

'Well, I did nothing. It was a pleasure to have you both with me for a short while. In fact, I'll now feel frightened to be alone here for the rest of the day.'

'It'll be all right,' said Berry.

It was about two o'clock. The broiling sun stood, almost immobilized, in the bare sky, pouring down its heat relentlessly. Through the trees on either side of the street, the white-hot rays cast shadows that looked like a grotesque jumble of spears, knives, and headless bodies of animals and human beings. The sun's blaze fell on the cow's carcass, on the blood drops near the tea-stall . . .

' I feel as though I've been through a baptism of fire,' Gautam said.

Berry merely nodded.

They now walked past the spot where, a few days ago, Gautam had seen a young woman vendor feeding her infant, while her customer leered at her nipples.

8

In 1946, a year before independence, the British rulers moved the Civil and Sessions Courts from their modest premises near the Kashmiri Gate to the new mammoth structure near the Azad Market to meet the mounting pressure of daily cases of civil disobedience against the government.

This complex of closely knit buildings looks like a giant beehive with a multitude of cells, each representing a different section of the law. The open compound that encircles the courts is cluttered with tea-stalls, stamp-vendors, typists—and touts who prowl about for gullible litigants, claiming direct access to the judiciary. Although the British christened the new courts Tis Hazari—the Mughal name for the halls of justice—the custodians of law always handed out their verdict in favour of the rulers.

Gautam came to the divorce court of Justice J.P. Appaswamy, with his lawyer, precisely at ten. Berry preferred to wait outside near a tea-stall in the backyard so that his presence inside the court wouldn't provoke Sarita.

A few minutes later, she arrived, accompanied by her lawyer. She was dressed in a gold filigreed Banarsi sari as if the occasion were a wedding rather than a divorce. Gautam dropped his head as soon as he saw her, striving hard to look disconsolate and lonesome as though he already regretted the foreknown verdict of the court. Berry had advised him not to look too confident lest the woman should change her mind even at the last moment.

Both parties had to wait for about three hours; it was only after lunch that the court crier announced their names. They were then ushered into the chamber of Justice Appaswamy, who was seated on a high chair, behind a lacquered table. Gautam noticed that the judge, who was in his mid-fifties, now looked fagged out. When Sarita's lawyer began to spin out his plaint, a mere mock show put up by both parties, the judge cut him short: 'I feel the learned counsel has meandered into irrelevancies. The basic issue is quite simple. The ground on which the petitioner is seeking divorce is her husband's conversion to Christianity. So I ask the learned counsel for the respondent if he wishes to contest this charge.'

'No, my Lord,' responded Gautam's lawyer.

'Then,' the judge moved in brusquely, 'I declare the marriage dissolved.'

As soon as the judgment was announced, Gautam rushed out of the court towards the courtyard where Berry was having his tea.

'Did you get it?' Berry asked him anxiously, putting down his cup.

Berry knew that in spite of the out-of-court settlement between Sarita and Gautam, she could have still ditched him. Having secured the transfer of the house in her name, wasn't she now in a supremely advantageous position to deny him the divorce? All that she had to say in the court was that she was still willing to stay with her husband even though he had changed his religion.

'*Mea culpa*!' Gautam exclaimed, throwing up his hands jubilantly in the air, like an athlete who finishes first in a race.

But hardly had Berry jumped forward to pat him on the back when someone shouted from behind: 'You prevaricator!'

It was Sarita, striding menacingly towards Gautam. 'You liar!' she bawled out again. 'The honeyed words you poured out the other day. I couldn't imagine you'd be so excited to get rid of me. And, there, in the court you looked so forlorn.' Then turning to Berry: 'And this accomplice of yours—isn't he a bone-breaker?'

Gautam felt tempted to even the score, now that he was a free man. His lips twitched out of revulsion for this woman. But Berry pulled him away.

'This is not the moment,' Berry whispered into his ears. 'Just stay cool. Let's get out of here at once. To Neel Kamal!'

While Sarita was still hollering, they both hurried away and took the first taxi on the road. Since it was too early for the cabaret, and the bar hadn't opened yet, they settled down to tea.

'I still can't believe I'm a free man,' said Gautam.

'It'll take you a little while to shake off the weight of those four years.'

'I guess so.'

When the bar opened, a couple of hours later, they took their seats near the cabaret floor. Gautam ordered a bottle of champagne and some pakoras. He felt the occasion now demanded nothing less than the queen of all liquors. When the drinks arrived, Berry raised his glass: 'A toast to your release!'

'Thank you.'

They both clinked their glasses. As the hall got filled up with people, the flashlights were turned on. They had hardly begun to drink when a cabaret girl swished onto the floor, like a comet. She was wearing only a see-through satin bra—that showed her breasts like two ripe mangoes—and a pair of gold-laced panties. Her long serpentine hair cascaded down to her thighs that glistened as the searchlight chased her from one end of the floor to the other. Then she broke into a voluptuous snake dance, crawling lithely as the music rose to a crescendo.

Her head touching the floor, she arched her supple body, like a swan—her thighs stretched taut, her breasts swinging like two inverted cups of nectar, balanced precariously mid-air.

A wave of excitement swept through the crowd—an upsurge of deep yearning for the body beautiful.

'Oh God!' Berry exclaimed. 'Isn't she a temptress?'

Gautam, however, looked staid, untouched.

'Is something still bugging you?'

'No, nothing.' Gautam just shook his head.

'Missing your wife?'

'Don't be silly.'

There was a pause. 'I was just thinking of that woman near the tea-stall,' Gautam said, heavily, 'nude and helpless.'

'Ah, the knight-saviour is reflecting on the brutality and

pathos of life!' Berry teased. 'Well, one has to move on . . . After all, I was there too. Don't be a bloody killjoy. We've come here to celebrate.'

'I'm sorry.'

'I tell you what's wrong with you, Gautam. You're a prisoner of your past . . . You must now learn to pull yourself together.'

'How?'

'Look at that girl's breasts. Don't you feel like swigging off those cups . . .?'

'Maybe I don't.'

'Come on, you sulking thing,' said Berry. 'What you need is a night with a girl like this dancer—to exorcize you. You'll then wake up the next morning a phoenix risen from the ashes.'

'There you go again,' said Gautam, 'as though a woman is only sex and a bout in bed could cure one of all tension.'

'Yes, it can old man,' Berry responded.

Someone from the back seat tapped Gautam's shoulder.

'Quiet please. Let the others watch the show,' the man hissed.

'Sorry,' Gautam said, turning back.

'Serves you right, my dear Gautam Buddha,' Berry whispered.

During the past few days, Gautam had begun to feel a sort of sexual impotence creeping all over him. He wondered if it was due to the trauma of betrayal. Should he allow Berry to talk him into something that was morally repugnant to him?

The dancer now moved into the final phase of her performance. She undid her bra to reveal the full rondure of her breasts. Then she slithered like a cobra from one table to another, sipping from every glass, kissing old men on their cheeks, the young ones on their lips. One bold creature even pulled her onto his lap, capturing her mouth in a fervent kiss. But she went pliant in his arms, taking it all sportingly.

When she came to their table, Berry stroked her smooth hips, saying: 'Won't you kiss my friend, please? He needs it most.'

But as the dancer bent over Gautam, he just looked away.

It was now time for supper.

'Will you get us something to eat, please?' Gautam asked a waiter, who appeared at their table.

'Some seekh kebab, raita, nans and hot chutney . . .'

'And some fried chicken,' added Berry

It was about ten when Gautam and Berry left the restaurant, flushed with a generous round of liquor and spicy food.

The evening was unusually tranquil, as though the rioters had taken a day off. The moon shone bright and clear in a cloudless sky, and although some heat still persisted, the atmosphere was no longer sultry. The traffic along Faiz Bazaar flowed smoothly. There were no military trucks rumbling down this main artery of the capital, no crowds on the pavements—only a few persons standing near the tobacconist's.

Both of them thought of rounding off the evening with Banarsi paans from the tobacconist, whose nimble fingers were folding up the betel leaves into neat little rolls for his eager customers. Above his head dangled a thin coir rope, whose smouldering tip served as an instant lighter for the smokers. His mouth stuffed with a paan, lips stained red and almost dripping with saliva, the tobacconist himself looked a perfect connoisseur of betel-chewing. His right hand dipped into each of the several tiny silver cups around him, containing a variety of coloured pastes. He took a pinch from each cup and rolled it all into a betel leaf.

As Berry pulled himself out of this small crowd, holding a packet of king-size Gold Flake and two paans, a middle-aged balding man, with bushy eyebrows and betel-stained teeth, drew close.

'Care to try some good stuff, sir?' he whispered.

Berry flashed a smile of understanding, while Gautam looked mystified.

'A virgin, sir—just turned twenty,' the man spoke again.

'I know it's always a virgin, even if the stuff is fusty.'

Gautam understood that Berry was talking to a pimp in his own language.

'This one's a real lotus, sir—fresh, untouched. Arrived only last week from the UP. And from a respectable family too.'

'A whole week gone and still a virgin?' Berry kept up his jibing.

'She had to be broken in, gently.'

'A Muslim?'

'Yes, sir.'

'And you?'

'A Hindu.'

'There's perfect communal harmony—isn't it?' Berry kept up his banter. 'And look, I'm a Hindu too, but my friend is a Christian—pure and tender like a lotus.'

The man looked a little nettled; he didn't relish this teasing.

'It's all right, sir,' he said, somewhat petulantly. 'If you're not interested, you don't have to needle me.'

But as the man was about to move away, Berry held him back by the arm.

'Angry?'

'No, sir. But I thought you were just fooling me.'

'On the contrary, we're interested in your stuff . . . Only, not tonight. We've had a gruelling day . . . How about next week—Saturday evening, eight?'

The man took in Berry with a probing glance, then smiled.

'All right, sir.'

'But do make sure she's a Muslim.'

Berry had a fascination for Muslim women who, he thought, were full-blooded because they fed themselves on such hot stuff as mutton rogan josh and seekh kebab, while most Hindu women were pale, anaemic creatures living on rice and lentils. Shyama he took whenever nothing better came his way.

'So two peaches, sir—one for you and one for your friend?' the pimp asked. He was eager to clinch the deal.

'But could you fix two virgins straightaway?' Berry asked, smiling. 'Why don't you let my friend have the first fling? I can wait.'

'All right, sir.'

Then turning to Gautam, Berry said: 'Your need is greater than mine.'

'Thank you,' said Gautam. 'But I am not interested in all this. Blatant prostitution doesn't excite me.'

'Don't turn on that holy stuff again, my dear. It's an honest deal. You enjoy a woman and she gets paid for it. Don't be a milksop.'

'What are the rates?' Berry now turned to the pimp.

'Twenty-five rupees for an hour plus the room charge—that's if you prefer it at the Bridge Hotel,' the man replied, announcing the rates as though he were running a grocery store. 'I guess, you know the place, sir.'

'I do,' said Berry. 'But what about the Kotla ruins?'

'No, sir. She's too respectable for that. No love in the open for her.'

'Sounds like she's something real special.'

'She is.'

'Then let's say two hours.'

'Okay.'

'Where do we meet?' Berry asked the pimp.

'At the Bridge Hotel,' the man replied, 'and I'll do the room reservation too.'

'Thank you.'

As Berry was talking to the pimp, Gautam suddenly realized that he'd been trapped. He stared at the pimp who looked menacing—bushy eyebrows, powerful hands and massive shoulders.

9

Since the Bridge Hotel is run in close partnership with Neel Kamal, most of its patrons comprise those who first visit Neel Kamal for food, drinks or cabaret, and then come here for a quick fling before returning home.

The hotel offers its clients exclusive privacy in its elegantly furnished rooms—spring mattresses, downy pillows, foam-leathered sofas and close proximity to the Kotla ruins. You may walk down the passageway on the second floor straight onto the terrace, from where you may climb up the tower to have a bird's-eye view of the southern part of the capital, stretching across a vast landscape, with the Delhi Gate on one side, the Red Fort on the other, and far beyond, the metropolitan railway station, a sooty, nondescript building with neon lights flashing the words: 'Delhi—Northern Railway.'

The Kotla ruins fascinate all visitors because of their legendary, romantic associations. They are the remnants of the royal guest house, the mehman khana, built by the medieval ruler, Feroze Shah, to accommodate his civil and military officers whom he summoned to Delhi, from time to time, on state missions, from other parts of the country.

Although he was himself an orthodox Muslim, a believer in total abstinence from sex and liquor, his officers often used this place for their orgies—eating and drinking—all through the night. Some of them would even take their women for a nocturnal boat ride on the Jumna, which then flowed only a mile and a half away. According to the legend, Feroze Shah never came to know how his mehman khana was misused for such revelry, so brazenly contrary to the Islamic principles of rigorous austerity.

Though the mehman khana survives today only as battered, roofless rooms, it still performs the same function as it did five centuries ago. Its tottering walls, just shoulder-high, guarantee transient privacy to any person who may bring his woman here for a brief hour or so, if he has no other place to use.

There is a tacit understanding between all visitors to the ruins not to encroach upon each other's territory in the midst of their individual operations. Of course, each couple has to announce its presence with a pair of shoes or something left at the open entrance of 'your room for the hour'.

The policemen prowl about at a discreet distance, outwardly ensuring law and order, but not without expecting a standard tip from each visitor. It is openly believed that most of them are on the payroll of Neel Kamal and the Bridge Hotel.

The hotel management has tried to recreate for its patrons the romantic atmosphere of medieval India. But the call-girls supplied by the Bridge Hotel are poor substitutes for the medieval nautch women who once entertained Feroze Shah's civil and military officers.

More out of curiosity to see the 'virgin' from the UP than to escort Gautam to the Bridge Hotel, Berry accompanied him to the hotel. When they arrived, precisely at eight, there was no sign anywhere of the pimp, or the girl. Only after some anxious waiting did they see a tonga pull up at the gate, and then alighted from this rickety vehicle the pimp and a woman in a black burkha. Muslim she presumably was, but Berry still wondered about this concealed creature. In any case, he decided to see the face before returning to Neel Kamal where he was supposed to wait for Gautam.

The pimp ushered both Gautam and Berry into the lounge, beckoned them to wait there for a while, and walked up to the Reception. Then he returned, with a smile on his face.

'Room number 204 on the second floor.' He addressed only Gautam. 'And now, please, fifty rupees plus thirty for the room.'

Diffident and embarrassed, Gautam pulled out his wallet and handed over the money.

'Will you walk up with this gentleman?' the pimp asked the girl, in a somewhat proprietary tone.

'But you haven't introduced *me* to her,' intervened Berry. 'Maybe I'll follow up too.'

'Sure, sir,' the pimp said, flashing his betel-stained smile. He whispered something into the girl's ears.

As though someone had touched a push-button, a delicate hand at once moved out of the burkha to uncover the face.

Indeed, the girl was astonishingly beautiful. Light wheatish complexion, a silver jhumka gleaming between the crescent-shaped eyebrows and dainty lips, like the petals of a buttercup. Since the head was still partially covered, only the lower part of her raven-black curls came tumbling down her shoulders. A luscious peach, Berry said to himself—and even if not a virgin, she was redolent of the fragrance and glow of a newly budded rose.

But, as the girl shot a glance at the two men, her eyes, deep and brown, looked wrathful.

'Oh God!' exclaimed Berry, hardly able to muzzle his yearning. 'I can now see,' he then whispered to Gautam, 'what I've lost to you. If the face is only a prelude to . . .'

'Calm down, will you?' Gautam said, himself fascinated by the beauty of the girl. 'We'll fix you something else, equally good. Now, will you go back to Neel Kamal and wait for me there?' He smiled.

'Oh, you lucky devil!'

As Gautam was about to take the girl away, the pimp, who felt pleased to have bagged two customers, said: 'Just two hours, sir. It'll be double for each additional hour, or for any part thereof.'

'All right,' Gautam said, dampened by the man's cold, mercenary tone.

'I'll wait in the foyer,' the pimp said.

It was a corner room on the second floor, which opened into the eastern wing of the passageway, leading to the terrace. As soon as they were alone in the room, Gautam said, pointing to the sofa: 'Won't you sit down there, please?'

'Thank you,' came the words, her voice just a murmur.

He himself began to pace up and down the room, fidgety and perplexed. Then he stopped near a window and looked back.

On the walls hung paintings of women, mostly nude, and coloured photographs of the erotic sculptures of Konarak and Khajuraho. In India, Gautam thought, there was no risk of violating any law of pornography, because Hindus worshipped the genitals, particularly the lingam, as fervently as they aspired to nirvana.

He'd hardly taken in the room when he saw to his great amazement, the girl already stripped and stretched out on the bed. As he looked at her entire body and not merely the face he'd glimpsed in the foyer, he felt entranced. Such a luxuriant, frank exposure of the body's harmony—the firm breasts, the slender waistline ebbing and flowing like a sandy dune, the shapely thighs, each like the creaseless trunk of a young poplar. It was a vision, almost mystical and ineffable.

'Would you like to come over, sir?' her feeble voice muttered. 'There isn't much time left, you know.'

The words came loaded with a frigid, disquieting ring. Her face, now sombre and tense, almost froze him. As he paced across the room, somewhat awkwardly, he stumbled against a coffee table and hurt his shin slightly. Then, sitting demurely on the bed, near her feet, he murmured: 'What's the hurry?'

Gautam couldn't bring himself to call her 'honey' or 'darling'. That would have rung out false, he knew. But, then, had he come here to make love or polite conversation?

The girl saw a flicker of bewilderment on his face. There was something unusual about this man. Otherwise, would he be sitting so bashfully on the bed's edge?

As for Gautam, his mind was in a whirl. What kind of girl was she? She couldn't be a virgin, for hadn't she unfolded herself with a sort of professional readiness?'

Suddenly, he became conscious of some incongruity in the situation—a beautiful girl stretched out nude in bed, and a sprucely dressed man sitting miles away from her. He'd never slept with any woman other than his wife, but having now been hustled into this, he might as well do something, he told himself.

'Have you been here before?' he asked.

It was only after the words had slipped out that he realized he'd blundered into asking such a question. Surely, he wasn't such a moron as not to see that he was with a call-girl.

'Twice.'

It was an impassive answer, devoid of any sense of shame. But the words sizzled with anger.

'Oh, I see,' he mumbled. 'I should have known.'

'Indeed.' The call-girl almost snapped back.

With a jerk, she gathered herself up in bed, clasping her arms round her knees. For a moment, the image of that other woman, standing nude on the pavement near St. John's, flashed through Gautam's mind.

'I don't know what you're up to,' she now almost glowered at him. 'Why don't you be done with it, instead of humiliating me . . .' she trailed off.

'Oh, I do apologize if I've hurt you in any manner,' Gautam replied, rising from the bed, and again walking away towards the window.

'Isn't time running out, sir?'

'Never mind,' he answered. 'You may dress up, please. Maybe we could meet again, another time . . . It's just that I haven't been able to bring myself to it . . . I'm sorry.'

Gautam looked out of the window at the open fields that sprawled all around like a chessboard—large squares of vegetable beds and here and there a tree, or a cluster of bushes. Far beyond, shimmered the waters of the Jumna.

'You seem to be so different from the others,' she said, this time in a tender voice; then reaching out for her sari which lay on the bedside table, she added: 'May I also ask you something, sir?'

'Yes, please.'

'Have you been here before?'

'Never.'

'And your friend?'

'Several times perhaps, though I've never asked him.'

Gautam walked back from the window and sat on the sofa chair beside the bed. The girl had already dressed herself and was reclining against the pillows.

'Are you from the UP?' Gautam asked.

'Yes . . . But how do you know?'

'The pimp told me.'

'Oh, Pannalal?'

'Is that his name?'

'Yes.'

'I'm very scared of him.'

'So am I . . .' she paused, suddenly realizing that she'd slipped up.

'Are you from Agra?'

In his mind's eye, he somehow associated her beautiful face with the Taj Mahal.

'No, Allahabad.'

The mention of the place startled him. He leaned forward from the sofa to probe her face. There was her unmistable resemblance with the bearded old Muslim killed near St. John's—the same arched eyebrows, the same chiselled chin . . .

'Haseena!'

The girl was taken aback. How did he know her real name when all the call-girls had been given new names? For secrecy's sake, to placate those customers who insisted on being intimate. She was, for instance, called Kaleema.

As her right hand brushed against her forehead, in utter confusion, the kumkum got partly defaced; it now diffused itself into a dull trail of mauve.

'Who gave you my name, sir?' she asked, dumbfounded.

'Isn't your father's name Abdul Rahim?' Gautam resumed, looking directly at her face. 'And isn't your sister's name Salma?' He paused. 'And don't you live in Mohalla Kashana?'

She was stunned. She took a few minutes to come to.

'How do you know all this, please?' she pleaded. 'Is my father in Delhi? He must have come after me. Tell me everything, sir—everything. You seem to know it all.'

Gautam's brow now darkened.

'Well, this is hardly the place or the time to tell you everything . . . I've only sad news for you—about your father.'

'Killed?'

'A few days ago. I feel terribly sorry . . .'

Haseena felt aghast, her pallid face twitched as she flinched under the blow. Then she turned over, buried her face in the pillows and started to sob. Gautam felt deeply pained to see her writhing in agony.

'Oh, my Abba!' she cried out.

'Please listen, Haseena,' said Gautam, tenderly. 'You'll have to take it bravely.'

'How did it happen?' A ghostly voice muttered.

'A Hindu mob got him. I happened to be there.'

'Oh, Allah!' she let out a muffled cry. Then she started sobbing again. 'How did you pick up my father's name?' she asked, a lump in her throad. 'And all about my family?'

'From an unmailed letter in his pocket,' Gautam answered, 'after the mob had abandoned his body . . . In fact, I've already written to your mother.'

'Oh God! How will she take it? . . . It may kill her.'

She sat up in bed, gazing at Gautam's face.

'I don't know how to thank you, sir,' she said, in a tremulous voice. 'You took the trouble of writing to my mother. That was very gracious of you. The news would shatter her, I know, but still . . . And here I am in Delhi—abused, humiliated—and now so brazened to any sense of shame.'

Gautam now understood the reason behind her prompt undressing; it was obviously a gesture of defiance against the world.

'Are you a Muslim, sir?'

'I'm now a Christian. A few days ago I was a Hindu,' he said. 'And I wouldn't mind becoming a Muslim. I don't believe in these religions—they all condone violence, instigate their followers to kill . . .'

'Yes, sir.'

'Don't sir me, please. Call me Gautam. That's my name.'

But she couldn't bring herself to calling him by name as there was something very dignified about the man.

'Are you a civil servant?' Haseena asked. Her eyes had partly dried up. She was now anxious to know something about this man.

'No, a journalist. I write for *The Challenge*. Do you read it?'

'Only casually,' she replied. 'At home we get *The Statesman*.'

'A much better paper,' Gautam said. 'Are you a graduate?'

'I was studying for my BA when I was whisked away from the college gate by some masked men. Pannalal's accomplices, surely.'

'What college?'

'Islamia.'

'I see,' said Gautam.

Now he understood everything. But there was no more time to talk. He looked at his watch and exclaimed: 'Just fifteen minutes more. Please get yourself ready. Our jailer must be out there waiting for us,' he said. Then, quite impulsively he asked: 'Is there anything I could do for you?'

'Can you rescue me from my captors, take me back to Allahabad?' There was a ring of humble supplication in her voice. 'It's very risky, I know. They could kill us both. I've been threatened with death if I ever tried to escape.'

'So you're living in a sort of concentration camp.'

Instantly, something flashed through his mind.

'Do you know the topography of this place?' he asked.

'Fairly well,' she whispered. 'I wish we had the time to go up the tower and have a look all around.'

'There's no time now, I'm afraid.'

They both looked at each other, their minds on the same wavelength.

'How about meeting here again,' said Gautam, 'say, next Saturday?'

A faint smile rippled across her face; for a moment she'd forgotten her pain.

'But what have you got for your money, Gautam?' The name now slipped through. 'Tears and words—and now a hazardous undertaking? An utterly losing bargain!'

As Gautam opened the door, there stood Pannalal in the passageway, beaming. Surely, his customer had had his money's worth, the pimp thought. But, when he noticed that Haseena looked happy, he felt somewhat disturbed. No, he didn't like his girls to get involved with strangers. That wasn't professional. This fledgling would have to be broken properly, he told himself.

'How did it go, sir?' he asked.

'Marvellous! I didn't have enough time, though.'

'You could have carried on, sir,' the man said, in his customary tone, 'no extra charge, of course.'

'Oh, well . . .' Gautam mumbled. 'Maybe you could fix me another round.' Gautam hated himself for using such vulgar language. But he knew that it was the only way to keep the man off the scent.

'Most certainly,' he said. 'The same girl or someone else? Why not try out another peach—equally exciting?'

Had the man become suspicious? Maybe that was the reason why he wanted him unstuck from Haseena.

'No, I might as well round it off with this girl, if you don't mind . . . Next Saturday then—same time?'

'Yes, sir.'

Pannalal asked Haseena to take cover under the burkha, and instantly she was whisked away.

A few minutes later, Gautam arrived at Neel Kamal. Berry was sitting with a foreigner, boozing.

'Meet Bob Cunningham,' Berry said, pointing towards his companion. 'An Englishman from Surrey. Works for Philips.' Then, turning to the foreigner, he said: 'This is Gautam. And haven't I told you everything about him already?'

Bob nodded smilingly.

'How d'you do?'

'How d'you do?'

Gautam glanced at the Englishman who appeared to be in his late thirties. But his chestnut hair, parted on the side, his slender moustache and an air of buoyancy about him, made him look much younger.

'Well, won't you both drop this how-do-you-doing?' said Berry.

'Yes,' said Bob. 'Imagine,' he added, 'we met just a couple of hours ago, and we've already hit it off.'

'And he has told you *everything* about me?'

'Yes.'

'And I assume you'd have told Berry *everything* about yourself?'

'Quite a bit, I suppose.'

'But that's most un-English,' said Gautam. 'You British always take time warming up.' Gautam plunged into an audacious informality, encouraged by Bob's openness. 'I often meet my English friends at the Press Club,' he continued, 'Mark Gwynn of the *Guardian*, Sylvan Baxter of the *Times*, Clive Ricks of the *Telegraph*—and they're all the same. Know any of them?'

'No,' replied Bob. 'Maybe I'm an exception, being part Indian. I didn't let Berry in on that. You see, my grandfather was born in Calcutta, and over the past several years, the family has been travelling back and forth.'

'So that explains your love of Indian food—rogan josh, hot chutney,' Gautam said, seeing the waiter bring in a tray loaded with spicy dishes.

'And dark girls—that's hot too,' Bob said, taking a large swig of his whisky.

'That's certainly most unusual,' said Gautam.

'Un-English again,' said Bob. 'Why, a divorcee has to keep himself going somehow.'

As Bob threw in these intimate details about himself, the other two felt still more closely drawn towards him.

'Well, Gautam is a divorcee too,' said Berry. 'I don't know why I didn't tell you that. But he's just a fledgling—only a few days old.'

'So we're two against one,' quipped Bob.

'But to Berry,' said Gautam, 'a wife is only an appendix. His main preoccupation is exploring other territories.'

'A wife's never enough, you know,' said Berry.

'Never!' concurred Bob. Then turning to Gautam, he said: 'But we've been waiting to hear about your great rendezvous. How did it go? How was she in bed?'

'Oh, you've been talking about this . . . Well, I didn't quite get there. I hope to do it next Saturday.'

While Berry looked a little mystified, Bob said: 'Tremendous self-control. You Indians can do the ropewalking with such finesse, balancing yourself between the Kama Sutra and the Gita.'

'It's a sort of yoga, you see,' Gautam said, inwardly

intending to tell Berry about Haseena, but only privately. 'It comes with arduous training—the art of turning oneself on and off any moment.'

Both Berry and Bob laughed.

'Was she dark?' Bob asked.

'There he lapses into darkness again,' Gautam said. 'No, she was of light wheatish complexion . . . But why this obsession with dark girls?'

'Maybe I've seen too much of light,' Bob said, smiling. 'So isn't it now time to try out some other pigmentation?' He paused. 'You know, Bill Thornton also has a fascination for dark girls . . .'

'You mean the police commissioner?' Berry asked, quite surprised.

'Yes,' Bob answered. 'In fact, we're both planning to go down south, to the Malabar Coast, on a holiday trip. If he ever gets off the hook . . . Not a moment's rest for him. Poor man!'

'Then you're quite close to the heart of the Indian administration,' Gautam said, also looking impressed.

'Or Anglo-Indian?' quipped Berry.

'That's not being fair to the man,' said Bob. 'In any case, we don't intend giving up on you. There are always ways of hanging on, you know.'

'That's clear enough,' said Berry. 'Lord Mountbatten, your Bill—and some English priests operating here and there.'

'But I'm neither with the bureaucracy, nor with the missionaries,' said Bob. 'I work for a private British company here, and I propose to stay on as long as possible. Because I love your country, in spite of its heat and dust.'

The waiter showed up again to ask if they'd like to have anything else.

'No please,' Gautam said, taking out his wallet.

'Let me take care of this evening,' Bob insisted.

'Very un-English of you again,' said Berry. 'Why don't we go Dutch?'

'No, I insist,' said Bob. 'In fact, I should very much like to have you both over at my house some evening. I have a fairly good cook, I think. But, let me assure you, it wouldn't be insipid British food—steam-boiled Brussels sprouts, mashed potatoes, scrambled eggs . . .'

'Thank you,' said Gautam.'

'And you'll meet a very special friend of mine,' said Bob.

'A lady?' asked Berry.

'Yes.'

'Indian?' Berry pressed on.

'Yes.'

'So you're already well organized,' said Berry.

'I guess so; otherwise, a divorcee's life in a foreign country could be awfully dull, you know.'

'Even on his own native grounds,' said Gautam. 'That's why Berry tried to pull me out of my blues.'

'But it didn't work out this evening, it seems,' said Berry.

'No.'

Berry looked at Gautam, puzzled.

As they stepped out of Neel Kamal, Bob offered to drop them home.

'Splendid,' said Berry. 'We should feel honoured to be escorted by a friend of William Thornton's.'

10

Two days after Gautam's encounter with Haseena at the Bridge, Delhi witnessed an unprecedented explosion of communical frenzy. A report in a local Hindu paper, *Our Land*, described in lurid details how a passerby had seen 'some members of the minority community' shovelling the mutilated carcass of a cow into the Shiva temple, near St. John's. The same paper carried an inflammatory editorial, demanding prompt action against the criminals, 'otherwise the Indian nation would feel provoked to wipe out those who, while living in our country, owe their allegiance to a foreign power.' The 'criminals' were, of course, the Indian Muslims and the 'foreign power' was Pakistan.

The paper then branded all Englishmen, staying on in India, as pro-Muslim, and accused them of acting clandestinely in collusion with the Pakistani spies. In fact, the highly incendiary tone of the article was directed as much against Muslims as against 'the British colonialists'. Lord Mountbatten, in league with Anglo-Indians and British missionaries, was alleged to be engaged in a diabolic conspiracy against 'our efforts to consolidate the fruits of freedom'.

'As for Mahatma Gandhi,' the paper commented, 'his self-professed saintliness wouldn't help us run the administration. His utterance that while he loves the individual Englishman, he is against all forms of imperialism, is too mild a protest against our erstwhile rulers, who had ruthlessly exploited our motherland for over two hundred years. How can we call him Father of the Nation when he has dedicated himself exclusively to the welfare of Muslims? While he should have stayed back in Delhi to participate in the celebration of our independence, he chose to work for the Muslims in Noakhali. His prayer meetings, at which he recites verses from the Koran, are an affront to our Hindu dharma. What has the Mahatma to say about the desecration of our sacred temples and the molestation of our women in Pakistan? If he persists in his one-sided commitment, he may soon have to pay dearly for it. In fact, his recent speeches and actions leave us in no doubt that he is itching for martyrdom, so that he may be ranked with Jesus Christ, Thomas Beckett and the Buddha.'

The paper went on to say: 'At this critical juncture, what we need is an Indian Jinnah, a Hindu Messiah, who would fearlessly weed out all treacherous elements from our Holy Land.'

The article concluded with the slogan: 'Har Har Mahadev.'

Althugh *Our Land* was immediately banned, some copies of the issue, carrying the inflammatory article, still dodged the police. Mimeographed leaflets of this editorial were secretly circulated all over the country. Within two days, India was in the grip of another cycle of communal frenzy. Thousands of Muslims were massacred, their houses burnt, and their property looted. Muslims too retaliated furiously.

In Delhi, William Thornton imposed a curfew from dawn to dusk. All public places—clubs, hotels, schools and colleges—were closed for two days. The curfew was lifted for only three hours in the morning to enable shoppers to pick up their groceries.

Ironically, as the communal violence spread, the weather cooled off. On the blackest day of rioting, the sky unfolded a large rainbow, all the seven colours laid out in sharply demarcated bands, like variegated silken pennons. Then poured down the rain, relentlessly, over the dead bodies of men, women and children rotting on the pavements, waiting to be hauled away by the police.

Gautam had told Berry all about Haseena and how he'd committed himself to helping her. Both of them now worked out a plan for the great rescue. But Gautam was caught up in a terrible anxiety. Would the curfew be over by next Saturday?

Fortunately, it was lifted on the third day, and as Gautam reached his office, his chief editor announced a special issue of *The Challenge* to expose the reactionary ideology propagated by *Our Land*. 'If India,' he said, 'was to forge ahead, she must shake off all religious bigotry. The basic issues involved were more economic than communal.'

All this fell in with Gautam's own planning. When he asked his editor if he could be sent to Allahabad, another hotbed of violence, to report on the scene there, and also do an article on communal harmony, his suggestion was readily accepted.

On Friday evening, as he sat on the divan in his room at Anand Parbat, piecing together his notes for the article, his mother walked in, looking flustered.

'Purnima's here to see you. I hope there's no more trouble for us.'

'What trouble, mother? You're such a timid thing,' he said. 'Now that I've got my divorce, what can that woman do?'

It was a subdued Purnima that shuffled in. She sat on the floor, near the window.

'What's the news this time?' he asked, sharply.

'All's well, sir.'

'Then why do you keep shadowing me everywhere?'

'I'm sorry, sir. I just came to see you.'

'Nobody ever visits for just seeing . . .'

Gautam kept up the ribbing, piqued by this woman's brusque intrusion.

'Sir, there was a wrangle between Mr Trivedi and Mohinder sahib the other day.'

'How does that concern me?'

'Mr Trivedi didn't think it proper for Mohinder sahib to visit our house so often. It was a sort of moral pollution, he said.'

Gautam felt amused to hear this pedantic expression. Since when had Trivedi been fired with the missionary zeal to ensure moral hygiene in his neighbourhood? Where was he when the romance was running at high tide during Gautam's visit abroad? Why had he started watch-dogging for him when it was all over? He felt tempted to ask Purnima if the neighbours had already heard about the divorce—Trivedi and the others. But that would have boosted her status as a confidante.

'Look, Purnima, I'm no longer interested in all this,' he said. 'Unless you have something else to say, I'm afraid I must get back to work.' And he picked up the pad on which he'd been writing his notes.

But she didn't budge. He now realized that he was somehow stuck with her for a while.

'I also came to know if you'd, please, let me work for you,' she said. 'I don't wish to stay with Memsahib any longer.'

Ah, the double agent, Gautam said to himself. Or, had Sarita suddenly become conscious that Purnima knew too much?

'But you already have a comfortable job—salary, saris, tips,' Gautam said, and he nearly added, 'the excitement of backbiting, muck-raking.' But he merely continued: 'I'm sorry we don't need any domestic help . . . My mother herself cooks for me, and this is a small house.'

'I could sleep on the verandah, in the kitchen—anywhere,' she said. Then, drawing a little close, 'I do plead guilty, sir—for several reasons.'

'What?'

Only after asking the monosyllabic question, prompted by his irrepressible curiosity, did Gautam realize how unwittingly he'd encouraged this woman to chatter on.

'The milk you daily had, sir, was always generously watered . . .' she said. 'And, sir, the other man—' she resumed, her face glowing to find in Gautam an intent listener, 'how you trusted him as your friend and colleague, and loved his child as your own . . . He used to visit her almost daily when you were abroad. He'd slip in from the front verandah, then stay on for the night. They'd have drinks in your bedroom. What things I've seen and heard! What gross betrayal! My heart bleeds!' Her eyes were now searching Gautam's face to see how he was taking it all. 'Oh God! How I've lived in sin all this time! If only I'd warned you earlier. Yes, I must take the blame . . . Only, occasionally, I used to have a word with Mr Trivedi. He's a good man, sir—very understanding, very helpful.'

Gautam nearly asked her to shut up at this point, but decided to let her flow on. Wasn't she spilling the beans?

'Now I wish to atone for all my past lapses,' the woman continued, 'by serving you.'

Gautam noticed how hard she was trying to bring up some moisture in her eyes, but it didn't work.

'She'll have to pay for all this,' the tape started running again. 'And pay very dearly too—that is, if there's any divine justice. In fact, already they've started quarrelling. Now she accuses Mohinder sahib of having a soft spot for you, because you came to see Rahul. Who else would have done anything like that? Sometimes I wonder if the person to really blame is Mohinder sahib or Memsahib. You did well, sir—shook off that piece of dirt . . . I doubt if the other man will ever marry her. It served her right . . .' She paused for a moment, then continued: 'She returned from the court the other day, thoroughly unhinged. She told Mohinder sahib how very jubilant you were over your release. Why not? While she'll now cry every moment—childless and husbandless—you'll have a hundred years of peace and happiness. What's the fate of a Hindu divorcee? Isn't she like a widow?'

What a devilish creature she was, Gautam thought.

How he'd been carried away by her avalanche of words. He wondered if a man's curiosity was any less than a woman's. If Satan had worked assiduously on Adam, our first man too would have succumbed to temptation. But, of course, the Devil found Eve more exciting, more vulnerable.

'Thank you for telling me all this,' Gautam said. 'But I've already told you we don't need any help. Please go away immediately before the evening deepens. These are not normal times, you know.'

What a damper on this loquacious woman! Purnima felt stung, deflated. As she rose to leave, her eyes were burning with rage and humiliation.

11

The next Saturday turned out to be quite calm—no arson, stabbing or rape reported by the media. It seemed as if the two days' curfew had let the frenzy cool off. Almost all the national papers, specially *The Challenge*, denounced the communal press. Nonetheless, William Thornton was not the sort of administrator to take any chance over a possible resurgence of lawlessness. Fire engines had been stationed at all vulnerable points, and mounted police patrolled the streets round the clock. With such a show of force, the public felt secure to move about freely. All clubs, hotels, schools and colleges were back to normalcy.

The plan had been worked out meticulously. Berry was to bring a handbag, with a couple of Sonali's saris and two changes of dress for him, direct to the railway station, buy the tickets well in advance, while Gautam manoeuvred his escape with Haseena from the Bridge. Gautam was aware that if the operation misfired, both of them might get killed.

Gautam waited for Pannalal and Haseena in the foyer, near the Reception. The girl at the counter flashed a smile at him. Yes, the man was waiting for his call-girl; perhaps she even knew the arrangement for the evening, Gautam thought. In this underworld, there were no secrets—members of this mafia shared everything.

As Gautam looked at the wall-clock, it showed twenty minutes past eight. Since eight, he'd been gazing restlessly at the swinging door; still no sign of Haseena and the pimp.

Surely the man had overheard his talk with her. And, if the pimp had also somehow come to know that he was a journalist, it would be a disaster. Perhaps Pannalal was aware that while it was possible to get around the police, it never worked with the press. These thoughts kept Gautam on pins and needless.

Suddenly, the door swung and there walked in the pimp and Haseena. Gautam nearly leapt forward to greet them.

'Sorry, sir, for being late,' Haseena said. 'We were held up near the Delhi Gate by a policeman, but Pannalalji somehow managed to palm him off.'

The pimp just grinned. Since there was no time to lose, it was Gautam who took the initiative. 'Here's seventy-five plus room charge, and another thirty for you, Pannalalji.'

The pimp understood that the deal had been struck for three hours this time.

'Thank you, sir,' he said, baring his betel-stained teeth. 'I've reserved the same room for you.' Then he added, with a leery wink in his eyes: 'Have a good time, sir.'

Gautam merely nodded. He had bought an extra hour to cover up any possible delay in taking off. He looked back to make sure that the pimp had settled down in the foyer.

As soon as they were alone in the room, Gautam announced his strategy. After a few minutes, she'd lead him to the terrace where they'd sit on the parapet for a while, then go up to the tower to survey the entire terrain.

And then they would take off. It might be a mile to the Ridge Road on the other side of the fields. With slush all around, they'd also have to wade through mud and swamp. It would be calamitous if they missed the 10:30 train.

'But, first, let me have a quick look out,' Gautam whispered. 'I've been having nightmares about your jailer.'

'He's been behaving rather oddly towards me,' she said. 'I hope he's not suspicious.'

Softly, he unbolted the door and peeped out. There was no sign of the man right down to the passageway's end. He must be drinking away in the lounge.

Gautam shut the door and said: 'The coast's clear. Now to the terrace!'

'Follow me,' said Haseena.

They stepped into the passageway, and through the rear door came to the terrace. As they sat for a few minutes on the parapet, Gautam looked all around, taking in the fields which stretched up to the southern end of Darya Ganj. Then they climbed up the tower.

From there, Gautam could survey the entire area. He could even see the turrets of the Mecca Mosque near Neel Kamal, the dome of the Victoria Zenana Hospital and, further down, the archway of the Delhi railway station.

'Now let me take over,' he said. 'I guess I've mapped out our route. About thirty minutes to the mosque, then on to the station—if all goes well.'

But as they were coming down the tower, a dazzling flashlight caught their backs. Then they could hear the footsteps of someone hurrying up from the eastern side of the terrace. Haseena looked back and at once recognized the face. It was Pannalal, closely watching their movements. So, the man was keeping them under his constant surveillance, from a discreet distance.

'There's the devil, Pannalal,' she whispered to Gautam, who felt frozen to the marrow of his bones. 'Put your arms around me . . . Hug me. Kiss me. Do something quick, please. He is not used to his customers just talking away.'

At once Gautam took her in his arms, bending over her mouth for a kiss. But he felt like an actor who has to do it under a blinding camera light, with the director shouting away: 'No, do it again . . . action!'

As he brought his mouth close to her lips, the footsteps faded away into the distance. The man had obviously felt reassured that it was only a sort of foreplay before the couple returned to their room for a bout of love.

'I guess he has now moved away,' Gautam said, his heart still pounding against his ribs. 'Well, it's now or never. I've spotted a strategic point to jump off the terrace onto the battered end of a wall, just knee-high.'

'Let's go.'

First, they softly paced towards the vantage point, Gautam's arm still clasping her waist. Then suddenly, he leapt off. With amazing promptness, Haseena too jumped after him. Now they were running breathlessly, across the fields, along the furrowed rows of cabbages and cauliflowers. But they'd hardly gone a few yards deep into the fields, when the flashlight caught them again. Then came a menacing cry: 'I'll get you both in a moment,' the pimp thundered. 'I'll suck your blood. I know what you're up to.'

The bald patch on Pannalal's pate gleamed like a sheet of Belgian glass in the candid moonlight.

As Gautam looked over his shoulder to see how close

the man was, he caught sight of the naked blade of a long knife, glistening above his flashlights. Then the sound of a splash. Their pursuer had slumped into a marshy spot which they'd cleared already.

'Keep running, Haseena! He's slipped . . . This may give us a lead.'

But she was nimbler on her feet than even Gautam himself, for she'd waded through a small strip of water while he was trailing behind, a little out of breath.

Ahead of them lay a shallow puddle, a remnant of last Thursday's rain, and then the main road which curved round the southern edge of Darya Ganj, like a sabre.

Gautam and Haseena sped along the road's edge, then turned sharply into a bylane. There they saw a house ablaze with a solitary fire engine fighting the flames. The sight of a huge crowd brough the couple some solace. They were out of danger; now they could easily thread their way through the mêlée and steer clear of Darya Ganj.

As Gautam was escorting Haseena through the crowd, he heard someone shout: 'It must be some bloody Muslim arsonist! We'll wipe out the whole lot of them.'

Another voice joined in: 'We'll pack them off to Pakistan.'

Then a maddening cry rumbled in the air: 'Har Har Mahadev!'

'Let's keep pushing ahead,' Gautam said to Haseena.

But just as he was about to get her out of the crowd into a bylane, Gautam's eyes caught Mohinder, who was standing on the compound wall of the burning house, a scrapbook in his hand. Was he reporting this incident?

Gautam had begun to seriously consider resigning from

The Challenge, if that was the only way to avoid seeing Mohinder in the offices of his paper. If the man turned around to see Gautam 'running away' with a young beautiful woman, wouldn't he report it all to Sarita?

'Is he someone you know?' Haseena asked, as she saw Gautam's eyes riveted on the man.

'Not really . . .' Gautam said, now shaken out of his thoughts. 'We must keep moving on.' Then, looking at his watch, 'We have only half an hour . . .'

'Do you think we'll make it to the station?'

'I hope so,' Gautam replied, leading her across the lane.

'Hey, Gautam!' someone shouted, jumping out of a jeep parked along the curb. 'What are you doing here? Reporting?'

It was Bala Subramaniam, special correspondent of *The Evening News*, and secretary of the Press Club.

'What a surprise!' Gautam exclaimed, taking the man's hand in a nervous clasp. 'I'm not reporting, Bala . . . But can you help me? I'm in trouble.'

'You do look flustered.'

'Can you take us to the railway station?' he asked. 'We're being pursued.'

'All right, get in both of you.'

While Haseena climbed into the rear, Gautam sat in front with Subramaniam. 'Eh, who's she?' Bala whispered into his ear. 'A real smasher!'

'A friend,' Gautam replied, smiling.

'Gallivanting?'

'I'm on a secret mission. I'll tell you later.'

The jeep leaped forward. In a few minutes they were at the station.

'Thanks a lot,' said Gautam. 'It was a question of life and death.'

'I'm glad I could do something for you.'

'Well, I shouldn't hold you back from reporting the fire,' said Gautam.

'It looks like you are on your way to some scoop . . . Good luck!' Bala waved to Gautam and jeeped away.

As soon as Berry saw Gautam and Haseena, he rushed towards them.

'Bravo!' he cried out, gleefully. 'But, look, what you've done to yourself. Splashed all over with mud.' Then, turning to Haseena he added, 'It must have been quite a sprint.'

'It was traumatic,' she replied, still gasping for breath.

Then, after a pause, Berry announced: 'I've some good news for you both . . . Two berths in a reserved coupe. A damned luxury these days, isn't it?'

'Great!' Gautam exclaimed. 'But how did you manage it?'

'Some name-dropping—William Thornton, for instance.'

'But you haven't met him.'

'I know his friend—Bob.'

Haseena stood by, now feeling relaxed and secure.

As they started walking towards the platform, Gautam narrated to Berry how they had had a close brush with death.

'Oh, God!' Berry said, looking quite surprised. 'Well, in that case, he may be still on the chase.'

'Yes.'

Berry then pushed a handbag into Gautam's hands, and

said: 'Why don't you both go into the waiting room and change into something better?'

A little later, the couple emerged, all spruced up. While Haseena was now draped in Sonali's sari and blouse, Gautam was dressed in a three-piece suit.

The platform presented a gruesome spectacle. The refugee special had arrived from Amritsar only an hour ago to unload hundreds of Hindu and Sikh refugees from Lahore, Multan and Peshawar—men, women and children. They were all squatting on the platform, huddled together, their hair unkempt, lips famished, faces moribund.

The Hindu Welfare Association had organized its camp in a corner of the platform itself, with ample supplies of medicines, food and clothing bought with the donations from the rich businessmen of Delhi. Some volunteers were even trained to give first aid for minor bruises.

But how could these volunteers help men with amputated penises, young women whose breasts had been chopped off after they'd been raped? It wasn't the physical pain so much as the social stigma these destitutes would have to endure for the rest of their lives. Their tales of suffering had incensed some of the volunteers to wreak vengeance. Frantically, they now prowled about looking for any Muslims on the platform.

Someone spotted a young Muslim couple trying to hide behind a newspaper stall. They were at once pulled out, stripped and knifed to death, their killers shouting: 'Blood for blood! Death to all Muslims!'

The platform presented a ghastly contrast—of exuberant compassion and heinous brutality. While some volunteers were consoling and distributing food and milk to the refugees, others were busy scouting about for Muslim victims. Word had gone around that the Howrah Express, carrying Muslim refugees from Patna, Lucknow and Allahabad, would arrive early next morning. So most of the volunteers were now keyed up for the attack. The train must be wiped out, they said: all young women whisked away and all men massacred.

And this must be done before William Thornton moved in.

Since Berry had been on the platform for about an hour, waiting for Gautam and Haseena, he'd witnessed several poignant scenes. Impressed with his stout body, a pockmarked young volunteer had even asked him to join them in the raid on the Howrah Express train from Calcutta, next morning.

'There'll be many young women, you know—and you may have the pick of them.'

'No, thank you . . . I just came to see off my brother and sister-in-law. They should be here any moment.'

'What a pity!'

'Maybe some other day,' Berry said.

'You'll be welcome any time. We're here day and night serving our Hindu brothers and sisters.'

Berry was discreet enough to hold back all this from Gautam and Haseena, who had already been through a great ordeal. So, he led them quickly across the flyover bridge to platform thirteen. But they'd hardly crossed over when the guard blew the whistle. At once they rushed towards the reserved coupé. While Gautam and Haseena jumped onto the train, Berry stood on the platform waving to them. Suddenly Gautam, who was standing near the door, clasping the handrails, cried out to Berry:

'Oh God! There he is—Pannalal!'

Berry turned round to see the pimp running along the platform, followed by a group of armed volunteers. While Gautam disappeared inside the compartment, Berry leapt on board, clasping the handrails.

'Is there any Muslim couple in that coupé?' asked the pockmarked volunteer.

Berry recognized him as the young man who'd asked him to join in the raid on the train, the next day.

'Don't you remember,' Berry replied, 'that I'd come to see off my brother and sister-in-law? I've just got them seated.'

'He's lying,' yelled Pannalal, drawing close to the train. 'There's a Muslim girl in there.'

The guard blew another whilstle, and the train jerked into motion. Berry asked the pockmarked volunteer: 'Why don't you look at the reservation chart out there?' Then, pointing towards a brown sheet of paper pasted near the door, he added: 'There, you may see the names—Mr and Mrs Gautam Mehta!'

The volunteer shot a glance at the chart, as he continued running alongside the train.

'It's all right,' said the volunteer.

'It's that man,' Berry now shouted to the volunteer, pointing to Pannalal, as the train was still inching out of the platform, 'There's a rabid Muslim for you—Abdul Hameed. Strip him and you'll see the circumcised devil.'

The entire band of volunteers now swooped down

upon the pimp. But before Berry could see him stripped, the train had chugged away.

'It appears I'll have to travel with you till Hathras, the next stop,' Berry said to Gautam. 'In any case, let me now make sure you have no more trouble.'

'Thank you very much for your help, Berry sahib,' Haseena said, regaining her composure.

'*Bhai sahib*—that should be more appropriate now that I've adopted you as my sister-in-law.'

Haseena nodded, smiling.

'Why don't you stay away from Neel Kamal for a few days?' Gautam advised Berry.

'Worried?'

'Yes.'

'I'll take care of myself,' Berry said.

As the train reached Hathras, the next stop, Berry jumped off, and taxied back to Delhi.

12

'A penny for your thoughts,' Gautam said, as he saw Haseena brooding, her chin resting on her right palm.

'Nothing,' she replied, now raising her head.

'There's always something to a mere nothing.'

'Well, how I have made you go through all this—for my sake,' she said.

'Maybe I've done it all for myself,' Gautam countered. 'Someday you'll understand.' He smiled.

'I was, in fact, thinking of my father,' she resumed. 'You see, today is his birthday . . . How some mysterious destiny controls our life rhythms.'

'Oh dear!' Gautam exclaimed.

'It's the living who are left to suffer,' Haseena said, in a heavy voice, 'while the dead are out of it all.'

'How true.'

'Because,' Haseena continued, 'the dead leave all their problems to others—and these others are sometimes complete strangers. Like yourself.'

'Maybe there's a mystic force that binds all humans together, dead or living, relatives or strangers.'

Haseena's gaze settled on Gautam's face; she was trying to fathom the meaning of what he'd just said.

The only sound audible in the coupé was that of the ceiling fan, whirring away above their heads, like a caged bird, fluttering helplessly against the steel bars. But the air it churned up was sultry; a sense of prickly stuffiness persisted even though the night had somewhat cooled down.

'Did they leave his body on the street, exposed . . .' Haseena's voice came on again.

'No,' replied Gautam. 'After the rioters left, his body was carried inside the church for a burial. I saw it all.'

'Then someday I may go and pray over his grave,' she sighed, 'even though he had a Christian burial.'

'What difference does it make to the dead?' Gautam said.

'You're so right.'

'And aren't there other kinds of death,' Gautam said, knitting his brows, 'worse than the body's extinction? . . . The trauma of betrayal, your wife's affair with your own friend and colleague, your son not being your own . . .'

'Are you married?' Haseena asked, her eyes searching his face for the clue to his agonized look.

'W-a-s!' Gautam drawled out the monosyllabic word as if to charge it with poignancy. 'I was divorced only a few days ago,' he said, with a lump in his throat, and then added: 'Remember the man standing on the compound wall of that burning house?'

'Who was he?'

'My wife's lover!'

'I understand,' she said, then drawing close to him, 'you've also been through hell.'

Hell—the word rang like a knell.

There was a moment's silence.

'But not darker than the one I've been through,' Haseena resumed. 'Imagine a group of young abducted girls, holed up in a house, murky as a dungeon, forced into prostitution at knife-edge. I don't know why I submitted myself to all that ignominy . . . But each time I let a customer take me, I felt as though I'd thrown a bone to a dog.'

'Then wasn't I also a dog when I came to take you at the Bridge?' Gautam asked.

'*No, no*,' she responded, repeating the word emphatically. 'You never touched me . . . you were a perfect gentleman.'

'I don't know.'

'But I am still baffled how someone like you could lend himself to such a situation.'

'It was Berry's idea,' Gautam said, 'to let me have some fun after my divorce . . . At first, I almost hated myself . . .' He paused. 'But now I think how fortunate I was to meet you . . .'

'Mysterious are the ways of Allah,' she said.

Both of them now lapsed into a long spell of silence as if they were listening to the train, hypnotized by its own thud-thudding, which had acquired a sort of musical notation—two accentuated notes followed by a pause. Outside the window, the trees on either side of the track looked like tall guardsmen in the pale moonlight.

Suddenly, the train screeched to a halt. As Gautam peeped out, he noticed that it was just a small wayside station with hardly any passengers visible on the platform.

A knock at the door.

'Who is it?' Gautam rose to answer.

'The attendant, sir,' a voice replied. 'Some coffee?'

'What station is this?' Gautam asked, opening the door to see a middle-aged man in khaki shorts and shirt.

'Besa, sir.'

Gautam looked at his watch; it was a quarter past twelve.

'Coffee?' Gautam turned to Haseena.

'This is hardly the time for it.'

'Then, let's wait till morning—for breakfast,' said Gautam.

'I can take the order for it right now, sir,' the man said. Then writing on his coupon, he asked: 'Two breakfasts?'

'He seems to have taken us for a honeymoon couple,' Gautam whispered into Haseena's ear.

Her lips curled into a smile.

'Breakfast will be served at Kanpur, sir, at seven,' said the attendant.

'Fine,' said Gautam.

As the man shuffled away down the aisle, Gautam said: 'Why don't you get some sleep, after that sprint? Tomorrow may be another hectic day.'

'Yes, I guess.'

'I'll take the upper berth,' Gautam said, looking up.

'Are you sure you'll be comfortable up there?'

'Sure,' he replied, rising from his seat.

Strange man, thought Haseena, so unlike anybody else.

In a few minutes, Gautam had gone deep into sleep. He dreamt that he'd strayed into a dark, narrow tunnel, over a rail track, winding like a python. He heard voices hissing all about his ears. As he kept trudging deeper into the tunnel, he lost all track of time. Was it day or night? And then as he heard a train clanging up from the rear, he stepped off the track, pressing himself against a wall, frightened out of his wits. He came to only after the train had whizzed past. He now lost all sense of direction—was he going north or south, east or west? A few moments later, another train sped past him, like an arrow shot through space. Again, he shrank back to the wall. This time the gritty surface of the wall scratched his back till blood came oozing from his shoulders. He then collapsed on the ground, and lay parallel to the track. But as another train shot through the tunnel, he recalled how, as a boy of six or seven, he used to place coins on the rail track to pick them up hot and flattened, after the train had gone by. He fumbled for some coins in his pocket, but it had many holes.

Then, suddenly, the tunnel was flooded with lights, hundreds of fluorescent bulbs glittering all around. As he gathered himself up, he saw, to his great amazement, that while the track had narrowed, the tunnel's belly had bulged, allowing him ample space to walk up and down. Then came jingling up the track, a toy train with seven bogies, each a different colour of the rainbow. It stopped at the spot where he now stood, dumbfounded. Out of the front bogie, some invisible hand held out a bunch of tuberoses, white and long-stemmed . . .

A knock at the door jolted Gautam out of his dream. As he climbed down to answer the door, rubbing sleep out of his eyes, he saw the attendant with a tray. Two breakfasts—and two roses.

'Doesn't he deserve a special tip?' Haseena suggested, turning to Gautam.

13

Finally, Purnima landed up at Gopinath's as a temporary maidservant, highly recommended by his cousin Padamnath Trivedi, for her 'competence, resourcefulness and devotion to duty'.

Purnima was, of course, happy to get a breather to look about for a permanent position elsewhere. Fired by Sarita, rejected by Gautam, the new job came to her as a boon. What had hurt her most was the callous manner in which Gautam had shoved her off.

All right, she said to herself, if he could be so insolent, she could also have him wound up a little. And now that she'd be working in a house near St. John's, she could somehow let the bishop in on how he'd manipulated to get his conversion certificate.

'Competent and resourceful' indeed she was, because within two days of her taking up the new job, she started hanging about the church. She'd stay back at the vegetable vendor's, facing St. John's, for hours together, hoping to run into someone from the cathedral.

Then it happened, on a pleasant, quiet morning. As she was standing at the vendor's, buying some vegetables, she saw a coffee-coloured man coming out of the church, carrying a jute sack in his right hand. As the man turned towards the shop, she at once placed him as a cook. In the community of servants, there's a kind of instinctive recognition of each other's status.

She didn't look too excited—only her fingers, which had been nimbly picking up crisp little peas as if they were rare green pearls, slowed down a bit.

'How're you this morning, Sam?' asked the vendor.

'All right, thank you.'

'I've some fresh potatoes for your master, and lettuce too. I've kept this stuff apart.'

'Thank you very much,' said Sam. 'He's been asking for the lettuce, specially.'

'Then won't you seize your treasure before somebody else takes it?'

The vendor pulled out a basket of fresh vegetables from behind his cushioned seat. It was obvious he'd hidden it away for his privileged customers only.

Purnima threw a side-glance at the dark man who was standing close by.

'May I also have some lettuce, please?' she asked.

'Sorry,' replied the vendor, 'it's all gone. I'd got it for the bishop only. Maybe next time.'

'I won't mind sharing some with you, ma'am,' Sam said, turning to her. 'You may take as much as you like.'

The voice was tender and gracious. Just the sort of man, she thought, she could use.

'No, I won't deprive your master of the lettuce,' she said, feigning to have changed her mind. 'I'll be around for a month or so . . . I can wait.'

Seizing the moment to introduce herself to the vendor and the servant, she told them how she'd worked for all sorts of people, her last employer being a journalist.

'I'm glad you'll be around,' Sam said, looking somewhat restive. She was wasting his time, he thought. He picked up his sack to move across the street.

But now determined to hold him back, Purnima kept the conversation going.

'You work for the bishop?' she asked.

'Yes, please,' he replied, rather impatiently, but he didn't wish to sound impolite. 'I've been with St. John's since I was a little boy. But the bishop is quite new to the church.'

'From Goa?' Purnima knew that most of the Catholic priests in Delhi came from there, or the Malabar Coast.

'No, he's an Englishman,' he said. 'And I wonder if you know an Englishman's weakness for potatoes and lettuce.' He threw in the last bit just to sound pleasant.

Purnima was aching to move in on some pretext. 'I'm sure your bishop knows my former master, Mr Gautam Mehta.' She now fired the first shot.

'Of course,' said Sam. 'Even I know him. He was baptized only the other day, at a quiet brief ceremony.'

'How much would your bishop know about him, really?' Purnima asked, a sneer in her voice.

'Not much, I guess,' replied Sam. 'He just came for the baptism. They discussed some theology, and I happened to bring in a soft drink for this gentleman.'

'That baptism,' hissed Purnima, 'it was all a sham. Just a rip-off, a big hoax on your church.'

'Was it?' asked Sam, somewhat puzzled.

'He did it just to get his divorce,' Purnima now charged

in. 'Change your religion and you get it in a jiffy—as simple as that.'

'Oh, Jesus!' exclaimed Sam.

'Don't you think your bishop should like to know all this?'

Sam looked befuddled. His fingers closed tightly on his sack full of potatoes and lettuce, as though it was the only stable thing he could hold on to.

'Father Jones,' muttered Sam, 'would feel terribly hurt to hear this.' Then he added: 'I wonder if an Englishman could ever plumb an Oriental's devious mind.'

Three days later, an old Austin pulled up in front of a house at Anand Parbat. Father Jones had picked up Gautam's address from the baptism register. But it was a different bishop; his sallow face now showed signs of inner disquietude and his hands, soft and sensitive, were shaking. Nervously, he knocked at the door, taking out his handkerchief to wipe off the beads of perspiration from his forehead.

Since Gautam's mother had gone out shopping, it was Shamlal who answered the door. He felt surprised to see an Englishman, in hood and gown.

'Is it Mr Gautam Mehta's house, please?' asked the bishop.

'Yes, sir . . . I'm his father. Won't you come in, please?'

'Thank you.'

Shamlal ushered the visitor in, motioning him to sit on the divan. In a flash, he understood who the man was.

'Is it Father Jones?'

'Yes, Mr Mehta.' There was a moment's pause. 'Since

you don't have a phone, I thought I could come without an appointment. I hope I haven't intruded . . .'

'Most welcome, Father,' Shamlal said, somewhat anxiously.

Shamlal was intrigued by the bishop's visit. Was it just a courtesy call to meet his son, a new convert?

'I'm sorry my son's out of town,' said Shamlal. 'He's gone to Allahabad for a few days on a special assignment. I guess you know he's with *The Challenge*.'

'I do,' said the bishop; then added, 'in fact, I happen to know a lot more about him than I should.' There was an edge to his voice. 'Maybe I should talk to you, instead of your son.'

'Yes, Father.'

'Is your son divorced?'

For a moment Shamlal felt as if he'd been hit on the head. But he soon managed to recapture his composure. With the bishop's brusque question, everything now fell into a pattern. Obviusly, someone had let the bishop in on the thing.

'Yes, Father. He got it last week.'

Shamlal proffered the additional information to show there was nothing to hide from anybody.

'Pardon me, Mr Mehta, but didn't your son use the church to get his divorce?' the bishop asked, raising his voice. 'Was it honest?'

Again, he pulled out his handkerchief to wipe the perspiration from his forehead. Nervously, he slipped to the divan's edge and nearly fell off. But he soon steadied himself.

'No, Father,' replied Shamlal, emphatically. 'He didn't abuse the church in any manner, if that's what you mean.'

'How?'

His sea-blue eyes stared quizzically at Shamlal.

'It was just a coincidence, speaking truthfully,' said Shamlal. But as he stressed the last word, he felt a lump in his throat. 'Believe me, he went to you out of his pure volition, in response to his innermost spiritual urges. He had it coming all these years. You may take my word for it, Father.' Shamlal paused, as though to recharge his mental battery. 'Let me tell you something. My son has always been a very independent young man, a loner. All my Hindu orthodoxy could never condition him. In fact, now it's the other way around. My own dogmatism has started cracking up under his influence . . . Do you know, Father, that in Lahore I used to hold public rallies against Christianity? Now I see everything in an entirely new perspective.'

The bishop regarded the speaker's face closely; he somehow felt overwhelmed by Shamlal's words, though he still looked a little perplexed. Seeing the bishop softening up, Shamlal moved in to nail it down.

'In fact, now I believe that Jesus was a sort of a yogi. Because he could control his physical agony on the cross.'

Father Jones moved closer to the speaker, deeply touched by this tribute to his Lord.

'Jesus never felt his own pain, Mr Mehta,' the bishop said, in a mellow tone. 'It was always the suffering of others that anguished him.'

'Precisely! Perhaps I now believe in Christ as another Hindu avatar, another manifestation of Vishnu.'

Father Jones felt exulted to hear all this. This was one of the most gratifying moments of his life.

'The real problem was his wife,' Shamlal now decided to play his trump card. 'She refused to go along with him.'

'Yes,' said the bishop, 'I do remember his telling me something about her.'

'So there was no other way except to split, gracefully.'

'Now I see.'

Seeing that he'd scored over the bishop, Shamlal now closed in. 'Excuse me, Father, but who told you about the divorce?'

'My servant got it from your son's former maidservant.'

'Aha!' exclaimed Shamlal. 'It's now crystal clear. That woman, Father, is a malevolent creature—a compulsive liar and thief. Fired by my son's former wife, she came to Gautam for a job. But in spite of his generous nature, he couldn't take her back. So now this viper goes about spitting venom everywhere.'

'I'm sorry I've caused you so much pain . . . Now I understand it all.'

As the bishop stood up to leave, Shamlal said: 'Won't you stay on for some tea, Father? My wife should be back any moment.' Inwardly, however, Shamlal was desperately eager to see the back of this man.

'No, thank you,' said the bishop. 'I'm afraid I must go now. Perhaps another time.'

'But you should come again, Father,' said Shamlal. 'It's been an honour to meet you. My house is blessed!'

But as the visitor walked out, he said to himself: 'Ah, the gullible Englishman!'

14

Independence gave Allahabad a prestigious position among the metropolitan cities of India. If Delhi was the administrative capital of the country, Allahabad began to function as its political headquarters.

Originally founded in 1583 by the Muslim emperor, Jalaluddin Akbar, and named by him as the City of God (al-Allahabad), it has witnessed the rise and fall of several dynasties. It has also been recognized as the confluence of diverse cultures, religions and languages. The massive fort that now towers above the bank of the holy Ganges was raised by Akbar around the famous Ashoka Pillar, bearing the Hindu emperor's edict of tolerance, peace and forgiveness. But, paradoxically, this fort became the scene of a cold-blooded massacre of several British families during the Indian Mutiny of 1857. Here, they were starved for many days before they were bayoneted to death in the presence of their English commander, who was then blindfolded and shot through the heart.

Independence saw the city again become an arena of violence. Since it had a preponderance of Hindu population, the Muslims here felt very insecure. Most of them had already fled to Pakistan, but those who stayed on herded together in small, cohesive colonies, scattered all over the city. In spite of the impassioned pleas of Maulana Abul Kalam Azad, the only Muslim minister in the Central Cabinet, and Jawaharlal Nehru's spirited denunciation of Hindu fanaticism in Allahabad, his birthplace, the Muslims here refused to stir out of their settlements and mix freely with other communities.

One such settlement was Mohalla Kashana, where Haseena's truncated family now lived—her mother, sister and uncle. In spite of the communal tension in the city, Haseena had, much against the advice of her parents, continued to attend classes at the Islamia College till she was abducted one afternoon, as she was walking back home in a burkha.

She was now returning to a fatherless home, with a Hindu—no, a Christian—she corrected herself. She couldn't foresee how she would be received by her family. Would she be discarded as a defiled thing, a fallen woman? Maybe her mother would have been happier, she thought, if she'd stayed back in Delhi, whatever might have been the circumstances.

The tonga they'd hired at the station suddenly pulled up at the Curzon Crossing.

'But we're going to Mohalla Kashana,' Haseena reminded the Hindu driver, who displayed a three-striped caste mark on his forehead.

'No, ma'm, I go no further,' snapped the driver. Then, after a pause, 'But aren't you Hindus?'

'Of course,' replied Gautam, intervening. 'We're just visiting a Muslim family there—old friends.'

'You can't be friends with Muslims any longer,' the driver shot off. 'They're all bastards, sir—fanatic Pakistanis at heart. Now that the Englishmen, their protectors, are gone, we'll take good care of them.'

The man had worked himself into a frenzy as though he was haranguing a large audience.

'But not every Muslim's bad,' retorted Gautam, 'nor is every Hindu a saint.'

'No time to listen to your idle sermonizing, sir,' the driver said. 'You'll soon find out the truth for yourself.'

Gautam paid him off brusquely and then helped Haseena out of the vehicle.

It was now Haseena who led the way towards Mohalla Kashana, which was just a few yards away. Stopping near a tea-stall, she asked him to wait there.

'You may have some tea or coffee. I'll be back soon.'

It turned out to be an hour's agonizing wait. Was she held back because of the mourning over Rahim's death, or was it the family's refusal to take her back? His mind was in a turmoil.

She showed up at last, but not alone. Gautam saw a man, in his late fifties, leading her up to the stall, with a small handbag in his right hand. Surely, she'd been bundled out of the house, Gautam thought—discarded and disowned. Immediately, he put down his cup of tea and briskly walked towards Haseena and her companion.

'I'm Haseena's uncle, Sheikh Kabir Ahmed,' the man introduced himself. 'We're very grateful to you, Mehta sahib.'

Gautam felt relieved to see that all his fears had been baseless. He raised his right hand to his forehead as a Muslim gesture of salutation, saying: 'I've only done my duty.'

'Not everybody does his duty these days,' said Ahmed; then he whispered into Gautam's ear: 'My sister is very eager to meet you. But since this mohalla is not safe for you, please change yourself into a sherwani and fez. It's all there in this handbag.' Then, pointing towards a public toilette around the street corner, he said: 'You may go in there.'

As Gautam emerged, Haseena felt amused to see him transformed into a 'Muslim'. Haseena was of course, already in a kameez and gharara.

'Thrice-born!' she exclaimed, light-heartedly. 'You certainly look magnificent in your new dress.'

'Do I?'

As the three of them walked past the tea-stall, deep into the mohalla, Gautam noticed many bearded blacksmiths squatting on the pavements, like street vendors. Bending over furnaces, they were hammering away—smelting, sharpening, fabricating. Nearby, on the bare ground, lay heaps of knives, swords, daggers, spears and hatchets. The place looked like an open arsenal of Muslim weaponry for defence against any possible Hindu raid.

'This is the other side of the coin,' Ahmed said, looking somewhat embarrassed.

'I understand.'

It was a small house—a bedroom, a drawing room and a small verandah. Gautam now salaamed Haseena's mother and smiled at Salma (it wasn't difficult to guess their identities).

'You've been a farishta to us, a guardian angel!' said Haseena's mother, asking him to sit near her on the sofa.

Gautam felt deeply touched by her generous compliment.

'Please don't embarrass me,' Gautam said.

'I received your letter only two days back,' Haseena's mother said. 'It shattered me. I haven't had any sleep since then.' Moisture welled up in her eyes.

'It's all Providence,' Gautam said. 'Man is only an instrument in God's hands.' But he soon realized that he'd spouted a platitude.

Outside, the hammer strokes continued: clang-clang, cling-clang, clang-cling.

'Indeed, my son.'

Gautam felt gratified to be addressed so endearingly. This emboldened him to strike a personal note.

'If you'd met my father, ammijan,' he was also impelled to respond with the same warmth, 'you'd have taken him for Haseena's father—such a striking resemblance!'

'Divine coincidence, maybe,' said Haseena's mother.

As Gautam now looked about the room, he saw on the front wall a silver-framed motto inscribed in gilded letters. Although he didn't know any Arabic, his knowledge of Urdu enabled him to guess what the words were. It must be the kalma, he thought: 'God is one, and Mohammad is His sole Prophet!' Close by, on the same wall, hung a coloured picture of the Grand Mosque at Mecca—a pleasing harmony of turrets and domes, in green, yellow and blue.

Gautam wondered how his Arya Samajist father would react to the kalma. Would he accept this monopolization of God by Mohammad as being his sole Prophet?

Into his stream of thought splashed a voice, wistful and poignant.

'It appears we will have to move—to Pakistan,' said Haseena's mother. 'Oh, the pain of getting uprooted from one's native place, after generations . . . But there's no alternative.'

'All of you?' Gautam asked.

'Naturally.'

How could he blame Begum Rahim for wanting to migrate?

'I understand your feelings,' Gautam spoke in a low voice. 'This subcontinent has become a savage battlefield. We seem to have lost our sanity. Nobody had foreseen the gruesome consequences of this partition. Not even Mahatma Gandhi!'

'Maybe the British knew,' intervened Sheikh Ahmed, who hadn't uttered a word so far.

'I'm not so sure,' said Gautam. 'I think we always tend to make them a scapegoat for all our lapses.' Suddenly, he became conscious of another presence in the room. 'What do you think, Salma?' he asked, turning to her.

'What?'

Salma's mind had been running in another groove. All the time she'd been watching Gautam intently, wondering if he was in love with her sister. Why had he done so much for the family? Although just a teenager, she'd matured within a few weeks.

'This idea of migrating to Pakistan,' Gautam now phrased his question more explicitly.

'Is there any choice?' came a soft but decisive reply.

'And you?' Gautam turned to Haseena.

'I don't know,' Haseena muttered. 'I haven't given any thought to it yet.'

'Oh,' said Gautam. Then, standing up, he added: 'I must get moving now.'

But it was only a feeler to see if they'd ask him to stay back for a while. So, he was immensely pleased when Begum Rahim said: 'Are you in a hurry?'

'Not quite,' Gautam replied, sensing he'd been liked by the family. 'But, tomorrow, I have to go around the city to report . . .'

'Yes, Haseena has told us about it,' said Begum Rahim. 'But you must take care of yourself.'

'I know,' he said. 'It should be all right so long as I move about in a dhoti and kurta, some caste mark displayed on my forehead.' He smiled. 'How funny, one's life depends upon what one wears these days.'

'Indeed,' said Sheikh Ahmed.

There was a brief silence.

'Would you please let me take Haseena along with me tomorrow?' Gautam asked Begum Rahim. 'I don't know the town so well. She could be a great help.'

'Wouldn't that be too risky?'

'We could do it in the same dress we came in from the station,' Gautam replied. 'A kumkum on her forehead . . . All that one needs these days is two sets of clothes in a handbag. It's like playing Dr Jekyll and Mr Hyde.'

Although only Haseena understood the literary allusion, the others were able to guess what it meant.

Begum Rahim pondered over Gautam's request; then said, gravely: 'I'll gladly let you take the responsibility.'

Had she given her consent out of obligation to her daughter's saviour?

'Thank you,' Gautam said. 'Then I'll meet her tomorrow afternoon, at the tea-stall, at two.'

15

Gautam was only a seventh grader, a young boy of twelve, when he first visited Allahabad for the immersion of his uncle's ashes into the holy Ganges. He still remembered how his father had argued with his mother, all the way from Lahore to this city, against such 'silly rituals'. He'd kept repeating that Allahabad was essentially 'a city of the dead', and therefore one of the most depressing places in the country. But since his mother had insisted on this ceremony, he'd given in, though most reluctantly.

One vivid recollection that had stayed with Gautam all these years was of an old, clean-shaven man, with a long fluffy tail drooping from the middle of his head, feeding three white swans on the holy bank. A small crowd had gathered around him, as though held under some divine spell. Since Gautam's father had gone to get some snacks, his mother felt emboldened to ask the man if the swans were his pets.

'No,' the man replied, 'these birds are the reincarnation of three pious *pandas* who, during their previous life, had served Mother Ganga as her high priests. Their souls have now returned to the holy river as swans, robed in these white garments. If you come here a little before dawn, you may even hear them chant mantras from the Bhagavadgita. At sunset, they fly away to parlok, the other world.'

But now, as a free-thinker, the Triveni appealed to Gautam's aesthetic sensibility only. The image of the two rivers, the Ganges and the Jumna, merging into each other, with the third river, the Saraswati, flowing invisibly underneath to forge the Triveni, merely testified to the fecundity of the Hindu imagination. No wonder, Hindus consider this confluence as the most sacred spot to immerse the ashes of their beloved dead.

As Gautam sat to lunch at his hotel, The Rainbow, a few yards away from the offices of *The Pioneer*, which was once edited by Rudyard Kipling, these memories kept bobbing up in his mind. Although the local press had predicted a calm day, he knew it could be just a lull after the communal storm that had rocked the city a few days ago. Maybe, the two communities were now bracing up for the next round. Hadn't he seen Mohalla Kashana already keyed up?

Precisely at two Gautam and Haseena met near the tea-stall. While she hastily put red kumkum on her forehead, he looked an orthodox Hindu in his white dhoti and kurta.

'You certainly got around mother very smoothly,' said Haseena.

'I had to do it, you know.'

'Where shall we go?'

'Anywhere,' said Gautam, somewhat excited. 'How about a trip to the Ganges? I've some childhood memories of the Triveni. In any case, rivers fascinate me—any river, anywhere.'

'All right,' said Haseena. 'But I'd be the first target there if someone sniffed me out.'

'With that kumkum, you look like one of the Hindu goddesses—Parvati or Lakshmi.'

'Do I?' she blushed.

'On the contrary, I'll have to watch out because I don't believe in all this crap—holy immersions, Triveni and all. I might give myself away, somehow. To me it's just like going to the beach. An afternoon picnic.'

'I've never gone deep into the river,' said Haseena, 'not as far as the Triveni. It was just a quick boat ride once, with a group of college students.'

'Let's do it then.'

Since they looked like pilgrims, they had no difficulty in hiring a tonga to the riverside. As soon as they got dropped there, they were besieged by a horde of *pandas*.

'A dip in Mother Ganga?'

'Want some holy water?'

One fellow was bold enough even to pull at Gautam's shirt-tail: 'This way, sir. Let me show you around.'

'Will you stop bothering me?' Gautam snapped. 'We'd like to do it on our own.'

Threading their way through a throng of pilgrims, they found themselves in front of a large shop which was cluttered with steel and silver bowls of various sizes, poised one on top of the other, like pyramids. The only other articles in the shop were tiny idols of gods and goddesses, in wood or bronze and, of course, picture postcards.

The shopkeeper was a clean-shaven man, plumpish and dark. Under his caste mark on the forehead, blinked two inquisitive, beady eyes. He was sitting on a wooden seat with nothing but a dhoti round his waist.

'Do you want some holy water, sir?' the man asked, coaxingly. 'Fresh from the Triveni.'

'No, please,' said Gautam. 'We should like to get it ourselves from the river.'

'Nothing like it,' the man said, looking impressed. 'But you'll need a bowl then. A silver one, I guess.' Without waiting, he reached out for a large silver vessel with a sliding lid, and the image of Lord Krishna engraved on the bulge. 'Only seventy-five rupees, sir. Very cheap. I may be losing a fiver on it, but I don't' care.'

'That's expenseive,' said Gautam; then, pointing towards a small stainless steel bowl, near the shopkeeper's right foot, asked: 'How about that one?'

'Only twenty,' replied the man, holding it up by the lid.

'That'll do,' Gautam said, taking two tens out of his wallet.

The shopkeeper's fingers grabbed the tens, which he nimbly clamped shut into a wooden cash box. His paunch quivered like jelly as he moved from one side to the other, showing three creases just above the navel. On his vast bosom stood some beads of perspiration, which he wiped off with a dirty towel. From his neck dangled a platinum pendant over his breasts, sagging like those of an old gorilla Gautam had once seen at the Wellington Zoo in Lahore.

'And won't you need two tickets, sir, for the boat ride to the Triveni?' the man asked. 'Well, the next launch leaves in about fifteen minutes—and just two seats left.'

This shop was obviously a multidimentional establishment, handling all sorts of transactions.

'No,' said Gautam. 'We'd like to take a small boat, entirely to ourselves.'

The man shot a searching glance at the couple. Surely, he thought, they looked special in all respects—urbane and aristocratic. Although Haseena hadn't spoken a word, the shopkeeper felt awed by her quiet dignity—and beauty. He took them for a newly married couple on their first visit to the holy city. That's why they wanted privacy.

'Then I'll fix up an exclusive boat for you.' The man said; then, swinging around, he shouted: 'Eh, Bhole! Where are you? Come out quick—will you?'

At once emerged from inside the shop, a mammoth creature, tall and muscular. Gautam noticed that he had three gold teeth, while the others were stained yellow with tobacco. He wore a pair of gold earrings and a gold ring. 'Lots of gold,' Gautam said to himself. Like his master, Bhole was stripped to the waist, and his body glistened in the afternoon sun, like a granite pillar.

'They want a special trip to the Triveni,' the shopkeeper said, turning to Bhole. '*Special*, understand?' He repeated the word as though he were relaying some secret message to his assistant.

'I do,' grunted Bhole. 'That'll be sixty only.'

'Isn't that a little on the high side?' said Gautam.

'Not at all, sir,' replied Bhole. 'That covers the entire ride—along the eastern bank, deep into the river, right up to the Triveni, then back via the fort. Sort of three-in-one. And an easy, smooth ride too.'

'We'll take it,' Gautam said, pleased with the itinerary. He felt too awed by this creature to get into an argument with him.

'Then may I have the sixty, please?' the shopkeeper stretched out his hand, like a performing monkey, asking for a handful of peanuts from one of the spectators.

'The entire sum in advance?'

'Of course.'

As Gautam paid up, Bhole leapt out of the shop, like a wild animal, beckoning his customers to follow him. A few yards down the lane, a swarm of beggars surrounded them—one-legged, armless, blind and those who were carried about in wooden trawlers by their partners. But they buzzed off the moment Bhole shouted them away.

Gautam and Haseena had to squelch through a patch of marsh before they got into a small, elegant boat, with a plank across the sides and two cushioned seats. A special arrangement indeed, Gautam thought. As the man undid the moorings, the boat lurched into motion. It was now gliding on the russet waters of the Ganges, occasionally ploughing through clusters of flowers, offerings of the living to the dead.

Above their heads, the sky hung bare and austere in the afternoon sun, whose reflection shimmered in the river like a golden bowl.

'Are you from Delhi, sir?' Bhole asked.

The bull's-eye! How could this man place him so correctly? But then, Gautam thought, he must have handled thousands of pilgrims from all over the country—from south, east, north, west. He felt scared lest the man should probe him any further.

Gautam was, however, now primed to parry off any further questioning.

'Yes.'

He thought a snappy, monosyllabic answer may discourage the man from getting any deeper into conservation. But hardly had he reclined against his cushion when Bhole broke into words again: 'We'll be at the Triveni in a few minutes.'

'Good.'

Well, Gautam thought, so long as the man talked like a tourist guide, he could endure him; but the *panda*'s loquacity was picking up.

'Newly married, sir?'

Ah, the primal assault! But by now Gautam was ready for anything.

'Yes.'

'So I've bagged it again.' He grinned, showing his gold teeth and sausage-like lips.

Now exulted, he pressed on, jerking his boat out of an obstinate whirlpool: 'What caste, sir?'

'Tripathi!'

Gautam knew it was coming, so he had it all worked out. He decided to feign Brahminism—just the bit he knew the *panda* would relish most.

'Ah, high-class Brahmin!' the man said, gleefully. 'Then you'd perhaps let me also do a prayer for you, at the Triveni.'

'Certainly.'

'Only five rupees extra.'

'That's fine.'

As the boat swung into the Triveni, the *panda* let it swirl around for a while.

'Now the prayer, sir?'

'Sure, go ahead,' Gautam said, feeling tempted to add, 'spit it out—quick.'

But Bhole came up with another question.

'Your father's name, sir—and yours?'

'My name is Lalit, Lalit Tripathi, my father is Girdharilal, my grandfather was Kishorilal, and I think my great-grandfather was Banwarilal. I guess this'll do.'

Gautam concocted an entire genealogical tree to give the irrepressible creature a mouthful of names to roll over his tongue.

'And your wife's name?'

'Seema, her mother's name is Kaushalya, her father's Kanhiya Kishore Pandey . . . I guess this would take care of her side too.'

'Splendid!' Bhole exclaimed. 'I feel very impressed, sir. You know, I've seen people who can't remember even their . . .'

'Father's name,' Gautam interjected, smiling.

As the *panda* began to chant mantras, interpolated with all the names doled out to him, Gautam recalled the other prayer he'd heard at St. John's, a few days ago. Father Jones and Bhole—what a contrast! While the *panda* was chanting away, Gautam's eyes caught the sharp borderline between the two rivers—a sort of silken ribbon separating the russet brown of the Ganges from the bluish green of the Jumna. He also filled up his bowl with the holy water.

Suddenly, the chanting ceased. Gautam wished he'd given this man some more money and a longer list of names so that he could have flowed on, like the holy rivers. But, having done the prayer, Bhole turned to him with a wry smile.

'Look at the colours, sir—the brown and the blue,' he said. 'The blue you'll remember was the colour Lord Krishna got from the great Naga when the reptile hissed out at him.'

'Yes, I know the story,' said Gautam; then, looking straight at Bhole's face, he asked, half-mockingly: 'What colour is the Saraswati that flows invisibly underneath these two rivers?'

The *panda*'s forehead wrinkled up; he'd never been asked this question.

'White, I think.'

'Why?'

'The colour of purity, chastity . . .'

Gautam marvelled at the *panda*'s nimble wit.

He then dipped his right hand into the Ganges and his left into the Jumna, feeling as though he was holding the two rivers within the palms of his hands. But it was the mythical Saraswati, flowing on in the subliminal zones, that really excited his imagination.

'How one wishes,' said Gautam, 'one could touch the Saraswati as well.'

'We can never touch things that are pure and invisible—God and Saraswati,' Bhole said, ponderously. 'But, now everything is being tainted.'

'What do you mean?'

'Muslims have descended upon us like locusts, defiling our temples, our sacred rivers . . . The other day, a Muslim couple visited Mother Ganga, masquerading as Hindus. But I got them in the end. Pushed them both into the river near the fort,' Bhole said, rolling his bloodshot eyes menacingly. 'I can always sniff out a Muslim.'

Startled, Gautam tried to look away, while Haseena blanched with fear.

'Last week, some Muslims threw a cow's head into the Hanuman Temple, near the Sapru Bridge . . .'

'Oh, that's too bad.' Gautam could mumble only a mild protest to appease the *panda*.

'But they paid heavily for it,' the *panda* said. 'We slaughtered two Muslim mohallas.' Bhole's eyes were flashing.

'Now the Muslim ringleaders are hiding away in Mohalla Kashana,' said Bhole. 'But we'll get them there too—sometime next week.' Then, looking at Gautam: 'Shouldn't a Brahmin like you also pray for us?'

'Sure,' Gautam replied, though inwardly shaken up.

Turning to Haseena, Gautam noticed that she'd gone death-pale.

'Is your wife unwell?'

'Yes,' he replied, helping Haseena rest her head on his right shoulder. 'We've had a long, tiresome train journey, you know. I must take her home immediately. Will you hurry up, please?'

'Certainly,' Bhole answered. 'But it's now just a few minutes to the fort. You shouldn't miss it.'

'I think we'll cut the fort. Some other time.'

'It's right there on the way, sir,' said the *panda*. 'You may have a quick look at it from the Jumna. A great fort built by Ashoka, but desecrated by Akbar, the Muslim bastard. If only we could snuff out all the Muslims from Allahabad, bring them to this fort and butcher them here.

That's how we wiped out an entire British garrison during the Mutiny.'

Gautam now realized how the rogue had worked himself into another tirade against Muslims.

Although Haseena had come to, her body was still quaking as though she had the shivers.

'But Ashoka's edict inside the fort preaches a different gospel, I think,' Gautam tried to soften up Bhole. 'Doesn't it exhort man to be tolerant and forgiving?'

'All that's gone now,' the *panda* snarled. 'In any case, Ashoka lost his head when he turned Buddhist. And are Buddhists Hindus at all?'

So the man had swept off Ashoka too under the carpet. Gautam wondered how the *panda* could talk of spiritual purity and massacre in the same breath.

Gautam and Haseena returned to the bank, their nerves totally shattered. They felt as though they had waded through a river of blood. Like a chamaeleon, Bhole had revealed diverse facets of his self—tough-muscled oarsman, Hindu priest and bloodhound. 'Three-in-one!' Gautam mumbled to himself, repeating the *panda*'s own phrase.

Bhole stepped out and began to pull the boat manually to the wharf; then he beckoned the couple to follow him through the marshy patch. But as Gautam tried to help Haseena out of the boat, it lurched, nearly throwing her off into the water.

'Watch your step, Haseena!' Gautam cried out.

Hardly had he uttered the name when Bhole sprang to his feet, like an incensed animal. Menacingly, he drew close to Gautam.

'Is she a Muslim?' he barked.

'What do you mean?' Gautam asked, utterly confounded.

'What was the name you just called?' The *panda*'s mouth was agape like a cobra's, its deadly fangs poised to strike.

'Seema, of course.'

Instantly, Gautam recaptured his mental agility.

'Haseena was what I heard, man,' the *panda* blared. 'And that name rings a bell . . .' He knitted his brows as if he was straining hard to recall something.

'Bholeji,' Gautam thought it prudent to address him respectfully, as a gesture of appeasement, 'surely, I should know my wife's name . . . I've never heard the other name. Who is Haseena? . . . Could you imagine a Tripathi going about with a Muslim?'

Gautam even tried to laugh it out, but he felt a cramping sensation in his stomach. Haseena kept looking about blankly, pale and shocked. Only vaguely did she feel that Gautam was fighting hard to retrieve the situation.

Bhole stood there petrified, finding it difficult to disbelieve what he had heard earlier. His eyes kept probing Haseena's face. She almost cowered under his ghoulish gaze.

The only thing that perplexed the *panda* was the kumkum on her forehead. And there stood Gautam in his white dhoti and kurta, holding the bowl in one hand and Haseena's arm in the other. They didn't look Muslim, surely. Or were they masquerading?

Before the man could say anything more, Gautam took out his wallet.

'Here's another tenner—for the prayer, Bholeji,' he said,

very ingratiatingly. 'We need your blessings for a happy married life.'

The man put out his right hand limply as if the tip didn't really excite him, his eyes still lingering on Haseena's face.

Although Gautam and Haseena tried to walk away composedly, inwardly they felt chilled with fear. What if the man got them from behind? They knew they must move on confidently till they merged into the crowd of pilgrims and beggars.

Gautam felt he would be turned into a stone if he dared look back—like Lot's wife.

As he dropped Haseena at the tea-stall, he said, 'Let's not meet for three days—till we get over this shock.'

She just kept silent.

16

As Shyama answered the door, she was surprised to see a foreigner standing on the porch—tall, golden-haired, elegantly dressed in a three-piece suit.

He enquired: 'Is Mr Dhawan there, please?'

Although the maidservant didn't know any English (except such words and phrases as 'sorry, please, yes, no, thank you, good morning and good evening'), she instinctively grasped the question. She would have readily responded with a 'yes, please,' had Sonali not showed up at the door.

'Please do come in,' Sonali said, surprised to see a white man.

'I'm sorry to barge in like this,' said Bob Cunningham.

From his accent, she understood he was an Englishman. How she wished some of her neighbours had seen her ushering into the house a distinguished looking Englishman. He was obviously a friend of her husband's. But shouldn't Berry have mentioned something about him? If she'd known about his visit, she could have put on her gold-embroidered sari and some special jewellery, though the French chiffon she was now wearing appeared sparkling too.

She looked about—thank God, the house wasn't too untidy. Fortunately, she'd got it done just that morning, otherwise she would have felt embarrassed over the smudgy glasspanes and orange peels strewn all over the floor. As for the piles of old newspapers and rags on the porch, how very lucky of her to have sold off the entire lot only last evening—at twenty paise a pound.

Sonali threw a side-glance at the visitor. Does it matter if a white man has his bath daily or not? Doesn't he always look clean? She caught herself imagining this man in bed, making love to his wife. Hair golden brown all over, body scented . . . she reined in her thoughts. Not for a Hindu wife to let her mind run wild.

Sonali led him to the drawing room.

'Hello, Bob!' Berry greeted him, almost jumping out of his chair, putting down his glass of rum on a side-table. 'What a surprise!' Then, pointing to the rum, he said: 'This is my afternoon round. How about joining me?'

'Too early for me,' Bob replied. 'Look, you don't have a phone, and I didn't note your address the last time I dropped you here.'

'Ah, the explanations and apologies,' said Berry. 'Back to your Englishness—appointments, phone calls. You're welcome here any time, Bob.'

'Still . . .'

'And that's my bride,' Berry said, turning to Sonali. 'Married seven years now, still my sweetheart.'

'Pleased to meet you, Mrs Dhawan.'

Bob understood Berry was laying it on too thick.

'Well, I'm in a hurry,' Bob's eyes returned to Berry. 'I just came to ask you, Mrs Dhawan and Gautam . . .'

'Sonali is the name,' interjected Berry.

'All right,' Bob resumed. 'I should be delighted if both of you and Gautam could come to my party next Saturday.'

'I'm not so sure about Sona,' said Berry. 'You see, she may have to visit her ailing aunt that evening. And Gautam's away in Allahabad . . . But I'll come.'

Sonali was left with no alternative but to give in to her husband's will.

'I'm sorry,' Sonali said. 'My aunt has not been keeping too well, lately.'

'What a pity!' Bob said. 'I hope she gets well soon.'

Why didn't Berry take her out anywhere? But she knew he was too tough for her. While she felt happy to be called a bride and sweetheart, inwardly she sulked at being left out of the party.

'Sona, darling, Bob should have at least a glass of beer before he goes . . .'

There she was, Sonali thought, just another maid in the house. For once, she wished he'd asked Shyama to bring in the drink.

As soon as Sonali walked out, Bob said: 'I wish you'd let her also come to my party.'

'Oh God,' Berry said, 'she'd have ruined my evening.'

Sonali brought in a plateful of popadom and a bottle of beer. Assuming that the two men would like to be left alone, she withdrew.

Taking the beer from Berry, Bob said, 'It's a great pity

Gautam won't be with us that evening . . . You know, I like him enormously.'

'He's away on a secret mission,' said Berry. 'Remember the girl he'd met at the Bridge?'

'Yes.'

'I guess he's fallen in love with her.'

'But wasn't she a call-girl?'

'Not really,' said Berry. 'She was a Muslim girl abducted from Allahabad. So he's taken her back to her family. Sort of freed her from her captors.'

'Interesting.'

'But this is not going to be smooth sailing, you know. For a Hindu to have an affair with a Muslim . . .'

'He'll come through all right,' Bob said, 'if he really loves her.'

'I hope so.'

As soon as Bob left, Sonali was back in the room, ruffled.

'You never take me out anywhere,' she sniffled. 'Am I just a servant?'

'No, my Sona, my dovey,' he cooed. 'It's just that Bob's party is likely to be much too boisterous. You don't know these Englishmen, my love . . .' He paused. 'But I'll take you to some other party. I promise—really.'

'It's always another party, another time.'

Berry took her in his arms, planted a gentle kiss on her lips, then pressing her close to his bosom, whispered: 'I love you.'

'I love you too,' said Sonali. 'But . . .'

'Would you like those foreigners to leer at you, my sweetheart?' he asked.

'Horrible!' she cried out. 'Please don't say such things.'

But she imagined how very exciting it would be to be hustled by a white man—so clean, so perfumed, so sophisticated.

17

Indians invariably come late to parties, but if they choose to impress their hosts, they can be awfully punctual too. Rather excited over the invitation to a party where he'd meet some Englishmen, Berry decided to make it precisely on time—eight o'clock. In fact, since he arrived at 17 Hastings Road a few minutes ahead of time (according to his watch, of course), he got off his taxi and began to pace up and down the lane next to Bob's bungalow. Then, as his watch showed 7:58, he adjusted his tie, smoothed the sleeves of his jacket, and briskly returned to the gate that displayed the name: 'Robert Cunningham.'

It was an old two-storeyed house—a spacious lawn in front, a side-path running down to the backyard, with a garage on one side and a servants' annexe on the other. Although the front lawn was somewhat dimly lit, the terrace was flashing with Chinese lights. Bob must have arranged the party up there, Berry thought, on a pleasant evening like this.

He now walked up to the porch, but he didn't hear any voices. Where was everybody else? He rang the doorbell and an old, turbaned servant, with a gilded belt round his waist, appeared at the door.

'Please come in, sir,' the servant said, in a typical British accent.

'Thank you,' Berry said, stepping into a luxuriously furnished lounge, with a high ceiling. 'Am I too early?' he asked the servant, glancing at his watch.

'No sir, it's about time,' came the crisp, polite reply.

But as he looked at the wall clock, showing a half-past seven, he realized that his watch was running too fast. So there he was, about half an hour before time! Never mind, he consoled himself. Wasn't he in the house of a friend?

He looked about the room. On the left wall hung a large reprint of *The Rape of Lucrece*, the ruddy, fulsome breasts and thighs of the woman glistening under the multilimbed chandelier. To the right was another painting, a Velasquez, showing a nude woman reclining on a couch, a hand mirror held close to her face by Cupid. So Bob had chosen the right sort of paintings for his house.

In a corner stood a huge piano, its glazed mahogany top glittering under a candelabrum of six uplifted arms. On one side of the closed piano lay a song book, half open. On the rear wall hung two large pencil sketches—one of the first East India Company ship that sailed to India and the other of the Victoria Memorial in Calcutta. Between these two sketches was a miniature, showing boar hunting in the deep forests of Rajasthan.

Berry felt quite impressed with Bob's palatial bungalow, its high ceilings, Persian carpets, rosewood chairs and silken tapestries. Feeling excited to claim someone like him as his friend, he thought, he'd now be awfully jealous of any other Indian getting anywhere close to him except, of course, Gautam.

'Omar!'

A voice boomed from the first floor. It was Bob's—deep and resonant, like an organ note.

'Yes, sir,' responded the turbaned servant, dashing up the steps.

A couple of minutes later, both peered down the banister.

'Is it Berry?'

'Yes, Bob,' Berry replied in a tone of exuberant informality.

'Is there anybody else?'

'No.'

'Then come right up, old boy, into my bedroom.'

Berry climbed up the steps.

'Aren't I a bit too early, Bob? . . . My watch is running fast.'

Berry hesitated at the door, expecting to be called in again.

'Come in,' said Bob. 'So this time it's your turn to spin out explanations and apologies.' As Berry stepped in, Bob added, 'I'm glad you're early. I can now introduce you to my friend. She must be somewhere in the dining room below, fixing things for the party. She's been a great help, you know,' Bob smiled.

'In bed too?'

'Of course.'

There was a moment's silence.

'What's her name?'

'M-a-l-a!' Bob let the name ring out like a church bell. 'Mala Patnaik!'

'Any other Indians coming?' Berry asked.

'No. Only my compatriots. All packed up to return home—to London, Liverpool, Glasgow . . .'

'So it's a sort of farewell party.'

'Yes, the play's done.'

'You know, Bob, they did a marvellous job here. I do feel sorry for them. I'm sure they're going to miss this bloody, hot country.'

'Miss?' said Bob, '. . . they're already feeling very low. A poor life awaits them out there. Meagre pensions, no servants, freezing winters—and the fog, the deadly, yellow fog.'

'Sounds ghastly,' said Berry. 'Then it was better here in spite of the heat and dust.'

'Any time. One can always beat down the heat with ceiling fans, khus-khus, and a little dust doesn't do you much harm,' Bob said, spraying himself with some perfume. He continued: 'I'm glad I'll be staying on for quite a while . . . An occasional meal at Neel Kamal and now friends like you and Gautam. Thank God, I'm not a bloody civil servant. I'm in business here, you know.'

'From here you may start another cycle,' Berry teased, though he felt touched by Bob's reference to him and Gautam. 'That's how it all began, didn't it? . . . First you came in as traders, then hung on—to rule.'

'Aren't we already working on the idea of equal partnership in the British Commonwealth?' He smiled.

'The same old game of diplomacy!' Berry said. 'No other nation can ever beat you in that, you know.'

'You got it, old boy,' Bob said. 'But, look, I forgot to mention that Bill may also join in, though for a short while only. You know, he's like a gynaecologist who may be called away to deliver anywhere, any time.'

'Who's Bill?' Berry asked, a little confused.

'Bill Thornton, your ringmaster, of course.'

'Oh, yes,' Berry said, feeling exultant at the prospect of meeting the great administrator, whose name he had used to manipulate rail reservations for Gautam and Haseena.

They both now came down the steps. Stepping into the dining room, Berry saw a beautiful young lady giving directions to a bearer. In a corner of an oblong table had been arranged spoons, forks in circular and pyramidal patterns, while at the centre stood a cut-glass flower vase. On a side-table, near a window, were placed several bottles of drinks.

'We'll have cocktails up on the terrace,' Bob said, 'and then come down to eat.'

Mala turned to see them coming in.

'This is Mr Birendra Dhawan, I guess,' she said, in a voice that was husky and sensuous.

'There, you see, she knows you already,' said Bob. 'Knows everything about you and Gautam.'

'And you're Mala Patnaik,' Berry smiled. 'I hope he's said only nice things about us.'

'Of course.'

Berry now looked closely at Mala. She was beautiful indeed—arched neck of a swan, limpid eyes of a doe and a mole on her left cheek. Even though her complexion was dark, her fawn-coloured sari had toned it down. Round her neck, she wore a fragile gold chain with a pendant of onyx. But what attracted Berry most was her ebony hair, rolling down her shoulders in a wave. Each time she moved her head, her long hair swung like silken tassels. Berry wondered how much sex there was in a woman's hair. Her choli, a couple of inches above her navel, revealed her belly down to the waistline. She resembled an Ajanta woman.

'And what has he told you about me?' Mala asked, her doe-like eyes dilated.

Before Berry could say anything, the doorbell rang. Looking at the wall clock, Bob said: 'Here they come! Pat on the stroke of the hour!'

The guests trooped in, almost in a procession, as if the same omnibus had unloaded them at Bob's gate, although each couple had come independently by private car or taxi.

There was Colonel Roger Lucas, formerly of the Third Gurkha Battalion, flaunting his perky brown moustache, and his roly-poly wife; Mr James Griffith, OBE, former deputy defence secretary, in his crisp Burton-tailored suit and his whippety wife; Dr Max Taylor, former medical adviser to the Ministry of Health, with his pallid wife; and Mr John Green, MBE, retired district magistrate, Ghaziabad, and his olive-complexioned wife. The last couple ushered into the lounge was the prematurely retired Major David Foster and his young pretty wife.

Since all the English guests knew each other, Bob introduced them only to Berry, Mala still being busy in the dining room. Although they beamed their complacent smiles, most of them felt embarrassed to meet an Indian whose presence, they felt, would be a damper on the party. But, then, everybody knew that Bob was utterly un-English, being something of 'an irregular', who enjoyed hobnobbing with 'the natives'.

The loss of the Empire had already left them embittered;

destiny, they realized, had pushed them out of their cushy jobs, and there wasn't much to look forward to in England. Thousands of them had already gone, hardly any Englishman wanting to stay back on his job under the Nehru Government. They'd much rather face hardships back home than lend themselves to the indignity of working under their Indian counterparts, whom they had bossed over till the fifteenth of August.

However, those who were attached to such commercial firms as Philips, Dunlop, Remington or Crompton, took the new situation as a great challenge. Some of these firms, particularly Philips, tempted their English officers to stay on in their jobs so that their Indian market might not slip into the hands of the American businessmen, who'd suddenly appeared in this part of the subcontinent as the most favoured foreigners.

Then there was a small minority of Englishmen—professors and principals in state colleges and universities—most of whom had taken roots in India. To them England would be an alien land.

'Would you all like to move up to the terrace for cocktails, please?' Bob announced. 'And then we'll come down for supper.'

The terrace had been brilliantly lit with Chinese lamps, and Crompton pedestal fans were whirring away at top speed to cool off the evening. Around a few potted crotons, with large spangled leaves, were arranged some chairs and tables in a semicircle. Near the parapet was a large table on which was arrayed a variety of Scotches—Dimple, Queen Anne, Black Dog, Jonnie Walker—along with Gordon Dry Gin, Hayward Brandy . . .

Since Mala was still downstairs, Berry was the only 'native' to move among these Englishmen. 'Transit passengers,' he mumbled to himself.

But as he looked at these white faces, glowing in the lights on the terrace, he couldn't help feeling impressed with their poise, solemnity and grandeur—traits he found utterly lacking in the new crop of Indian civil servants. Berry was indeed happy at his country's freedom—but at what price! Like his chief engineer, most Indian bureaucrats were vindictive, mean, conceited, tardy at work and irrepressibly corrupt. The Gandhi cap was now an 'open sesame' by which flew open all the portals of power.

Carrying his glass of neat Dimple, Berry walked over to the major's table, attracted by his young beautiful wife.

'May I join you, please?'

'Certainly,' replied Major Foster. 'Lovely weather—isn't it? Not too oppressive.'

There it was, an Englishman's perennial obsession with weather, Berry thought.

'Yes, it isn't too sultry.'

'We really don't mind the Indian weather at all,' the major said, as though speaking on behalf of his wife as well. 'We'd prefer it to the vile British winter—blizzard, mist and smog.'

'Yes, I guess.'

A brief pause.

'It's a great pity we have to leave India,' Foster resumed, rather wistfully, looking away at one of the Chinese lamps. 'I came from England just two years ago. We got married at Agra and now . . .'

Berry picked on Agra as a convenient point to keep the

conversation running, while he threw a furtive glance at the major's wife.

'A beautiful city—Agra,' said Berry. He used the adjective for Mrs Foster rather than for the city of Shahjehan.

'The Taj by moonlight—fascinating, isn't it?' said the major.

'Do you know the romantic story behind this peerless mausoleum?' Berry asked.

'Yes, we do,' Mrs Foster joined in. 'We got it from the Blue Guide. Emperor Shahjehan's love for his beautiful wife, Mumtaz Mahal.'

'Oh, you remember even the names—that's great,' Berry said effusively, as his eyes rested momentarily on her bosom.

'That must be the Viceregal Lodge, I guess.' Berry heard Colonel Lucas say to Mrs Griffith, at the next table.

'Of course,' responded Mrs Griffith.

They all stood up and moved over to the northern edge of the terrace as if to get closer to the Lodge.

'And is that one of the Lodi Tombs?' Mrs Green asked her husband, pointing in another direction.

'Don't be silly, darling,' he replied, in his gruff, magisterial voice. 'The Lodi Tombs are miles away from here, right there in the western sector,' he added, pointing towards another part of the city.

Mr Green's face, after his third double Scotch, was deeply flushed, and his voice now wobbled. As for his wife, her immediate concern was to locate the western sector.

All other eyes were now focussed on the Viceregal Lodge, resplendent with neon lights. Every three minutes, a revolving searchlight grazed its dome, as though inviting attention to this erstwhile seat of imperial glory.

'I wonder how Lord Mountbatten is taking it . . .' said Dr Taylor. 'He certainly looked a trifle jaded in a press photograph I saw the other day.' He spoke authoritatively as if he'd personally examined the first governor-general and found him rather anaemic.

'He seems to be doing jolly well,' Colonel Lucas said, now gone quite tipsy. 'But doesn't he owe his new position to Edwina and Nehru? You know what I mean.' But the others let this pass.

Suddenly, they heard the sound of a siren on the road; then a flagged car zoomed into Bob's bungalow, followed by a jeep.

'Oh, the police commissioner!' exclaimed the colonel.

Excitedly, Berry looked forward to meeting William Thornton.

'My apologies for being late,' the commissioner said, as he appeared on the terrace. 'Oh, this blasted job! Not a moment's rest.'

Berry watched him intently. He was a handsome man, in his early forties—tall and wiry, his curved brown moustache adding an awesome dignity to his face, which wasn't all white. Had it been a little toned down by the dullish pigmentation of his Kashmiri mother? Obviously, the two shades hadn't quite interblended. But his hair was golden brown, and his eyes had the bluish tint of the British Channel.

'It must be distressingly nerve-racking, Bill, to be on the run all the time,' said the major. 'I mean your daily dose of arson, rape and killing.'

'Nightmarish!' Bill exclaimed, the word ringing loud in the air. Bob whisked him away to the bar.

'What's your poison, Bill?'

'Gin with tonic' he said. 'Yes, I need lots of tonic. All kinds too.'

Since the commissioner knew everybody else, Bob took him over to Berry.

'Meet Berry—Birendra Dhawan—a very dear friend.'

'Very pleased to meet you,' said Bill.

'You came quite close to my locality,' said Berry, 'when you controlled the mob fury in Pahar Ganj, about ten days ago.'

'Oh, that terrible fire!' said the commissioner. 'It was a rotten affair . . . Do you know, Mr Dhawan, who started it?'

'A Muslim from a nearby mosque,' Berry replied. 'That's what the papers said the next morning.'

'Not at all!' said the commissioner. 'It was a Hindu who did it. It's always a Hindu who throws a cow's carcass into a temple, and a Muslim who dumps a pig's head into a mosque . . . Diabolic ingenuity, isn't it? The idea is to keep the battle raging.'

'Very intriguing,' said Berry.

'Let me tell you another thing, Mr Dhawan,' the commissioner resumed. With a double gin, his tongue had loosened up. 'My control room has just picked up a message from Allahabad. It seems that some Hindu pilgrim was killed right on the bank of the Ganges, and his body thrown into the river. Now I'm absolutely certain that it is a Hindu's doing, and soon you'll have another round of communal violence there. And, well, there may be a retaliation in the capital.'

'How interesting,' Berry said. 'But there is an area in Delhi where both Hindus and Muslims operate in close partnership.'

'I don't quite get you.'

'I've heard,' Berry said, 'about a brothel behind Neel Kamal, in one of those bylanes shooting of Faiz Bazaar, where they keep abducted girls, mostly Muslim, from all over the country. I got it from a waiter at the restaurant, a couple of days ago. And to cap it all, they operate in collusion with the police.'

'Shocking!' the commissioner burst out, as he helped himself to another gin. 'Can you give me some idea about the location of this place, please?'

'That's all I know, I'm afraid.'

'I must get there somehow,' the commissioner said, with a ring of determination in his voice. 'That place needs cleaning up.'

'How much can you clean up, Bill?' interjected Mr Griffith, the former deputy defence secretary.

'I don't know, sir,' replied the commissioner. 'It's an awful mess, no doubt.'

'Well, we must now leave it all to you and Lord Mountbatten,' said Mr Griffith. 'We'll be gone next week.'

By now everybody had gathered around the bar to listen to the commissioner's account of crime in the capital.

'What I can't understand is how all this is happening in the land of Buddha and Gandhi,' said Mrs Taylor.

There was a sting in her voice as though she were accusing the entire subcontinent for its lapse into barbarism—in spite of its professed cultural heritage.

'But haven't we had our own wars of religion?'

intervened Bob. 'What about our Chambers of Horrors, heretics burnt at the stake? Human nature is prone to violence everywhere, East or West.'

'The Original Sin?' muttered Mrs Green.

'I wouldn't go that far,' replied Bob, 'but there it is, the stark reality.'

The conversation froze when Mala appeared on the terrace, dressed in a crimson silk sari, her hair cascading down her shoulders. So she had her special wardrobe in Bob's house, Berry wondered—saris during day, and perhaps negligees at night.

Although Bob's English friends had heard about his liaison with 'a native woman', nobody had seen her before. So when Mala came up to announce supper, they were all surprised to see a lady of great elegance and charm. Mrs Foster, the major's young wife, felt a stab of jealousy to see all eyes now turned towards the Indian lady.

'Ladies and gentlemen,' said Bob, 'if you wish to propose a vote of thanks in advance, here's Mala. She's done it all . . . I'm just a guest like anybody else here.' He smiled.

'I haven't done much, really,' she mumbled, blushing.

As the guests started to move down to the dining room, Mrs Foster whispered into Mrs Green's ears: 'Is he going to marry that dark thing?'

'Don't you know he's somewhat touched in the head,' replied Mrs Green. 'He's capable of doing anything crazy. Look at his letting loose this native amongst us—this Cherry or Berry . . .' Both sniggered.

Hardly had they started the first course when the phone rang.

'It's for you, Bill,' Bob said, holding the receiver in his right hand.

'Some problem, I'm sure,' Bill said, rushing to the phone.

As he finished talking to his control room, he turned around and said: 'I knew they'd do this to me. I couldn't be so lucky as to have an evening off . . . It's blasted arson this time. A cinema hall gutted near Asaf Ali Road.'

'What savagery!' said Mrs Taylor.

'It seems they were showing some Hindu movie,' Bill said, 'one of those religious fantasies . . . But I know who must have done it. A Hindu!'

As he was about to walk out, Mala said: 'Mr Thornton, you must have a bite before you go. Just a little something. Won't you have some meat biriyani, please?'

And, instantly, she started filling up a plate with roasted chicken, fried rice and kebab.

'Thank you,' said the commissioner. 'But I don't think I should delay. This could lead to a serious riot. Anything.'

And in a few minutes, he drove out of the bungalow.

'Poor man!' exclaimed Mrs Griffith. 'No peace for him.'

The party continued late into the night as the guests started drinking again after the supper. Then Bob played some of his favourite songs on the piano. As he finished, Mrs Foster said: 'Let's all sing "He's a Jolly Good Fellow",' and everyone broke into the chorus.

18

Sitting in a cane chair, on the balcony of his room on the sixth floor of his hotel, The Rainbow, Gautam let his eyes rove about, listlessly. Down there, some distance away, a huge buffalo lay in a dirty pond. Then a crow flapped down from a nearby tree, perched on the animal's back and dipped its beak into the water to drink up. Gautam almost winced as if he felt the crow's spiked claws on his own back. So he felt relieved when the animal turned on its side and swished its tail to whisk the bird away.

To his left, far away near the horizon, Gautam recognized the central tower of the fort he'd briefly seen the other day, in the course of his boat ride with Haseena. Near its base shimmered the holy waters under the tropical sky of early September. To his right flowed the traffic, along a winding road—tongas, pushcarts, rickshaws and taxis.

Suddenly, an image crystallized before his mind's eye—Haseena's face, young, beautiful and innocent. An indeterminate emotion now welled up in his heart. How he wished he'd actually kissed her on the Kotla terrace! But it would have been an act done under the pimp's uncanny surveillance. And then the long talk about the living and the dead, throughout the train journey. How the body wilts away under some mental pressure.

For the past few days, he'd started to entertain serious misgivings about his potency. Could he really make love any more? Hadn't something dried up within him? Sarita's betrayal and her ceaseless nagging had done it to him, surely. So, maybe, that was the reason why he'd given in to Berry, to try it out with a call-girl. But the fates had willed otherwise . . .

Engrossed in these thoughts, Gautam dozed off in the chair.

Suddenly, he felt some dark pressure on his lips. As he opened his eyes, there she was—Haseena! She was kissing him.

'You?' he almost cried out, as he sat up in his chair, his eyes dilated in utter amazement. 'How did you get in?'

'Your door wasn't bolted.'

'Oh, I must have left it that way,' he said. 'How did you find my room?'

'From the Reception, of course.'

'But I'd advised you not to stir out of your house for at least three days . . .'

'I couldn't stay away from you.' She smiled. Then, after a pause, she said: 'Won't you come into the room? It's rather warm out here.'

Gautam now moved into the room and sat on the sofa. She nestled up to him, and rested her head on his left shoulder.

'How did your mother let you come, Haseena?'

'She knows I have to help you with your assignment.'

'My assignment?' He laughed, now folding her in his

arms and kissing her impetuously—her mouth, her cheeks, her earlobes. 'This is it!'

Haseena's fingers now began to work on the top button of his shirt, which didn't come undone so easily.

'Oh, these nuts and bolts!' She beamed. 'Maybe I should rip off this obstinate thing.'

'Why don't you?'

They now moved over to the bed, near the sofa.

As she flicked off the button, it went rolling across the carpet, like a white bead. Then a vibrant hand started rippling up and down his chest, creating ripples in his bloodstream. His temples and his earlobes began to throb. He felt he could almost hear his heart leaping, like a dolphin out of some bottomless sea.

A man's passion is whetted hundredfold when he feels that he is intensely desired by the woman he loves, that her passion is more overwhelming than his own, that in the act of love she scores over her male partner.

As Gautam's chest came bare, showing a tenuous wisp of hair round his nipples, she started kissing him all over, from his throat down to the groin, till he felt he couldn't hold himself together any longer.

'How about you?' he murmured, his heart pounding fast. 'Still bundled up in layers within layers of your sari?'

It was now Gautam's turn to discover her body almost for the first time; not the one she'd offered him at the Bridge Hotel.

Like a young apprentice in love who has promptly learnt his lessons, Gautam began to taste the flavour of her body, drinking off at every fountainhead. The two bodies now sparked off each other, caught in a frenzied rhythm of love—the ebb and flow of wanton breathing, of touch and go.

As they lay halcyoned in each other's arms, light as rose petals, Gautam thought about the genesis of love—how Adam might have savoured Eve's body for the first time, after she'd tasted the forbidden fruit. It must have happened one evening, casually, as the first humans lay alongside each other on a bed of myrrh and myrtle in the Garden. Then it was perhaps Adam's hand that inadvertently touched Eve's breasts, arousing her to some blind inner fury.

A wave of exultation rose within Gautam; then he felt as though his body was winding down, and he was coming down a giant magic wheel that had carried him up midair. A delicious languor now crept into his brain. He dozed off.

When he awoke, Haseena was gone. There was no trace of her anywhere.

Then his eyes fell upon a letter on his desk, clipped in a hairpin.

Dearest Gautam,

Since you've gone into a benign slumber, I wouldn't even dare kiss you goodbye. That would be a sort of sacrilege. There you lie on the bed, breathing heavily, naked and defenceless, like a babe.

Yes, I love you—very much. I couldn't bring myself to speaking it out, like so many other things I should like you to know. The written word can be such a comfort since it's a sort of smokescreen to cover up the brazen exposure of the spoken word.

I want to be with you always, everywhere. I've decided to tell mother about it. No more subterfuges for me. Doesn't lying taint the soul? Salma has been asking me about you. Mother and uncle, I think, have already guessed something about us. But now they'll all know directly from me . . .

In fact, I've become quite fearless. I'm no longer frightened of the panda, or Pannalal. What will be, will be. There comes a moment in one's life when one just wants to be. Perhaps it's also because I've now come to believe in fate. How else would you have come into my life—and in those circumstances?

So I'll let things take their own course. Let's see how and when the panda's men would launch the raid on Kashana. Remember, how that man was startled to hear my name? He's surely a racketeer, a member of some mafia. But I can now take them on, Bhole and Pannalal, single or jointly—if I have your love.

My only regret is that I couldn't come to you as a virgin. But if virginity is as much a state of the body as of mind, I felt this afternoon like a nun who renounces her church to take a man she's fallen in love with.

I feel I should let you have two days to work on your assignment—your article for The Challenge. In any case, I'll be busy all Friday when the family will offer a special namaz at the Medina Mosque for my father's soul.

So take care, my dearest, till Saturday. I'll be waiting for you at the tea-stall, at two.

Only yours,
Haseena

PS: Since you wrote to my mother in Urdu, let me share these verses with you, from a ghazal by a local poet, now migrated to Pakistan:

Let there be no talk of pain
For this moment of peace has dropped
With the summer rain—
  Drink it up!
  Let all our yesterdays be cinders.
  Come, my soul, let this moment stir
  Us into a new ectasy
  Known only to angels
  For they commune not through words alone.

19

For the next two days, Gautam remained under the spell of Haseena's letter, reading it over and over as though it were the gospel of love, till each word of it had etched itself on the tablet of his memory. Well, if he wouldn't be able to see her till Saturday, he told himself, he might as well start working on his article on communal harmony.

But his mind, still preoccupied with Haseena, refused to settle down to writing. Then, on Friday morning, something flashed across his mind—why not use the Ashoka Pillar in the fort as a convenient symbol to organize his ideas on the subject? Since he'd also planned to pick up his mail at the General Post Office (in case Berry, his father or his editor had wanted to contact him), he could easily walk over from there to the fort, which was only a short distance away.

So after lunch, he put on his dhoti, kurta and khadi jacket (since he knew he'd be moving about in the vicinity of the holy Ganges), and got into a tonga. Reaching the GPO, he saw a large crowd of people doing their postal chores. It was after a long wait that he got to the general counter for poste restante, behind which stood a tall, snub-nosed man doling out mail to people in the queue.

Gautam received two letters, one from his father and the other from Berry. His father wrote how tactfully he'd handled Bishop Jones who'd come on a sort of fact-finding mission. 'It seems his servant learnt from Purnima how you'd used the church for your divorce. But don't worry. I have explained away everything. However, you should call on him when you return, even attend a couple of Sunday sermons to take the edge off his suspicion.'

The letter from Berry was just a casual thing. He wanted Gautam to 'have a good time. But don't overdo it, old boy.' Then he mentioned how he was looking forward to a party at Bob's, on Saturday, for which he'd personally come to invite him. 'Surely, there'd be some white stuff there.' The letter ended: 'Don't feel too anxious about me. I'm keeping myself miles away from Neel Kamal. Only once did I stop off at the tobacconist's for a Banarsi paan, but after making sure that Pannalal was nowhere around. And that's where I learnt that the pimp was out of station. "Gone to meet his relatives," said the tobacconist. So just relax.'

As Gautam stood on the steps of the main entrance, holding the letters in his hand, he became conscious of someone watching him. It was a man sporting a jockey cap, the front flap pulled down across his eyes.

First, the man lingered near the telephone booth, as though waiting for his turn to make a call, then he moved over to a column in the central hall. Somehow Gautam felt intrigued by his movements. Why was he constantly switching from one place to another? Was he waiting for someone to finish his postal chores so that he could join him? Or maybe, Gautam thought, he was subconsciously still being haunted by Bhole. But if it was the *panda*, he would have certainly recognized him in spite of the hooded face.

Gautam put the letters into his pocket, shook his mind off Father Jones and the *panda*, and began to walk towards the fort. A few people had already started moving in that direction.

Suddenly, the sun broke through the slit of a large cloud, and the ground began to glisten like a sheet of glass. A sense of uneasiness descended upon everybody. But since Gautam was at the head of the trail, he felt happy to enter the fort before the heat became unbearable.

He stayed inside the fort for about an hour and a half, gathering from his guide (who kept lecturing away almost like a professor of history) all the information about the triple-faceted Ashoka Pillar, with its Hindu, Muslim and Christian associations. He was shown the spot where the British had been massacred during the Mutiny, and the Pyramidal Tower from where one of Emperor Akbar's Hindu wives used to watch the Triveni before saying her morning prayers.

It was, however, the Ashoka Pillar that interested him the most. Alongside the famous edict, engraved in Pali, was given the English translation, on a separate plaque:

> True religion does not recognize any barriers
> Between one human being and the other. It embraces
> all living creatures—man, animal and bird.
> Compassion, endurance, understanding and love are
> man's greatest treasures.

Here was the vision of an ancient Indian emperor. Gautam wondered if the hate-torn India of today would respond to this message of love and peace.

By the time he came out of the fort, it was late afternoon, but the sun was still holding forth in all its fury. Ominously bare, without a shred of cloud, the sky was throbbing with the white glare of heat.

Since there weren't any trees around, Gautam walked down the steps to the fort's base, near the bank of the Ganges. He now sat on a rock, in cool privacy. He'd wait there, he thought, till the scorching afternoon deepened into evening.

Soon he felt that his mind was losing contact with the human world. Far away he saw the Triveni, the silken borderline between the two holy rivers. However, it was again the transcendent Saraswati that gripped his imagination. He fancied a white stream flowing under the Ganges and the Jumna, unseen and untouched. He knew it was a mere illusion, a hoax played by *pandas* on the gullible pilgrims. But now he willingly surrendered himself to this fantasy. Hadn't this belief somehow held the minds of countless generations of Hindus? Here they came with the ashes of their dead, and prayed for their rebirth as humans. Indeed, the invisible was always more potent than the visible—that's why the Saraswati claimed supremacy over the Ganges and the Jumna. As he sat there musing, a whiff of breeze wafted across the waters, ruffling his hair. It was bracing, tranquil and cool.

Suddenly, he heard the muffled footsteps of someone inching closer towards him, and then a shadow lengthened across the rock on which he was sitting. Perhaps it was someone like him, Gautam thought, looking for a quiet spot. But, instantly, he noticed the shadow of a man wearing a jockey cap. He was startled; but before he could get to his feet, the man had already emerged from behind the rock. And there he was—Pannalal! As the pimp now took off his cap, Gautam saw his balding head, his bushy eyebrows. He was holding a long knife in his right hand—all primed up for the assault.

Gautam went pallid with mortal fear, cold sweat appearing on his forehead.

'So here we meet again, sir . . .' the man grinned, baring his betel-stained teeth. 'I saw you heading for the fort. I took the longer route to let you first do some sightseeing. Liked the fort?'

'Oh!' stuttered Gautam.

'Thank you for choosing such a quiet spot for our reunion,' said Pannalal; then added, 'Where's she?'

'I don't know.'

Gautam looked about desperately to find some avenue for escape, but he felt helplessly trapped this time. On one side swirled the russet waters of the Ganges, on the other loomed the man.

'Looking for some way out?' he growled; his upper lip pursed in a sneer. 'Not a ghost of a chance.' He paused. 'Unless you tell me where she is . . . I've contacts on the river, and nobody would tell where your body was thrown. So will you speak out? . . . Where's she?'

'I've already answered.'

'Don't forget,' he said, gnashing his teeth, 'I can still spare your life, if you let me know.'

'Perhaps it's one of the Muslim mohallas,' Gautam

mumbled, now thinking it prudent to keep the conversation running to gain time.

'Which mohalla? . . . Baradari, Ibadat, Meena or Kashana? I've already checked at the first.'

'Meena.'

'You're dodging me. You're wasting my time,' he blared, lunging with his knife towards Gautam's left shoulder, ripping off his shirt. Blood began to drip from his collar bone.

A film appeared before Gautam's eyes. He almost staggered on his feet.

'There, you see,' the man resumed, 'your crimson blood is greeting you. Touch it with your right hand and feel its fresh warmth . . . I'll wait till I get the right answer.' Then, raising his voice to a threatening pitch and pointing his knife at Gautam's throat: 'Haven't I waited long enough? Your friend had me stripped on the platform! . . . Yes, I knew you'd come to the General Post Office for your mail, visit the fort or have a dip in the Ganges. How could you be in Allahabad and miss the Holy Trinity? See, how very patiently I've waited for my moment. It's my turn now. If you don't tell the truth, I'll make minced meat of you. Understand?'

'It's Mohalla Meena, truthfully,' Gautam replied, looking death-pale. His right hand now felt the blood seeping through his kurta.

A streak of pain shot through his body.

'What house number?'

Pannalal looked a little interested, now withdrawing his knife from Gautam's throat.

'House number eighteen, lane four. Just behind the butcher's shop, opposite the Tibbia Clinic.'

Gautam had regained his mental nimbleness, in spite of the pain that was now racking his shoulder. A plethora of details would do it, he knew. The game of numbers!

As Pannalal was lapping up this information, his eyes probing Gautam's face, a large lizard crept up through the sand—its translucent belly panting with heat, its tongue flicking in and out of the air. It stopped for a moment as though looking curiously at the two men.

The crinkle of the lizard crawling over a dry leaf sounded in Gautam's ears. The creature was now moving towards Pannalal. It was a harmless thing, Gautam knew, still . . .

'A snake!' Gautam cried out, pointing towards the lizard.

Since Pannalal had also heard the rustle, he turned around sharply to see.

In a flash, Gautam leapt forward and kicked the man in the stomach with all his frenzied strength. The pimp reeled, his knife dropping out of his hand. Instantly, Gautam picked up the weapon; then, pouncing upon him, like a wounded leopard, he plunged it into his heart.

A piercing cry, and the pimp slumped on the ground, his blood streaming into the sand.

And then, as he let the knife drop from his hand, Gautam felt as though he had had a stroke of sensory paralysis. Momentarily, his ears were muffled and his eyes darkened. It was only after a while that he realized he was still alive, while the other man lay dead at his feet.

Indeed, he'd lied himself out of death, just as he'd lied to get his divorce. But wasn't lying justified in certain circumstances? After all, the only sin was the lie that tainted the soul—not the one which only counteracted evil itself.

But while lying may be sometimes justified, how could one condone one's killing of a human being, howsoever evil? He recalled how, as a small boy, he used to listen to his father reciting verses from the Gita, dramatizing the argument between Prince Arjuna and Lord Krishna, the former hesitating to kill his own kinsmen on the battlefield, while the latter exhorted him to kill them for a noble cause. In any case, Gautam said to himself, he had had to choose between killing or getting killed.

He now saw himself standing over a dead body, oblivious even of his own bleeding shoulder. What if someone caught sight of him there red-handed (and indeed his hands were blood-stained), even though such killings were now daily occurrences all over the country? Still, he mustn't let the dead body lie there exposed to the vultures. So mute and helpless did Pannalal look in death that he now felt compassion for him, not hatred.

Slowly he dragged the corpse across the sand and then pushed it into the river. Only after it had been swept away on the crest of a wave did he break into a sort of insane laughter. Gazing at the palm of his right hand, he said to himself: 'Look, hand, what you've done! I thought you could only write, hold a book, a glass of wine, or pick up morsels of food . . .'

He dipped his hand into the river, but the blood lingered on the fingers. Rubbing it a couple of times with sand, he immersed it again in water to see all the stains gone. Then, tearing off the sleeve of his kurta with his right hand, he bandaged his own wound tightly.

He now started walking towards the rear gate of the fort to reach the main road where he hoped to find some taxi or tonga. Fortunately, he found a lone taxi near the traffic lights.

'Can you take me to some clinic, please?' he asked the driver, who was puffing away leisurely at his cigarette. 'I've been stabbed—just a few minutes ago. Hurry up, please—will you?'

The man, his caste mark showing prominently on his forehead, jumped up, recognizing Gautam as a fellow Hindu.

'It must have been a Muslim, sir?' he asked.

Gautam merely nodded and beckoned him to start the engine.

'Oh, these villains!' the driver exclaimed, turning on the ignition. 'I'll take you, sir, to a very good Hindu doctor.'

The doctor was equally solicitous; immediately, he dressed up the wound.

'You're lucky,' he said, giving him an injection and some pills, 'nothing serious at all. Just one dressing should do. These pills are for pain, whenever you feel uncomfortable.'

When Gautam offered to pay him, the doctor shook his head.

'Not from a victim of Muslim stabbing,' he said.

Nor would the taxi driver accept any fare. Such generosity, Gautam said to himself—but towards one's co-religionists only!

Back in his room at the hotel, Gautam felt as though he was falling apart. For most of the night, the horrible scene kept dancing before his mind's eye.

Next morning, *The Pioneer* carried the story on its front page: 'A member of the majority community was brutally killed last evening, by a member of the minority community. It came to light only when the body was washed ashore, near the southern wharf. The victim was identified by Pandey Bhole Ram as Pannalal, a pilgrim from Delhi. The authorities are taking every possible precaution to prevent any outbreak of violence in retaliation. Armed police have been posted in such sensitive areas as Mohalla Baradari, Ibadat, Meena and Kashana.'

While Gautam felt amused to see how the killing had been attributed to the Muslim community, he now understood the sinister link between the pimp and the *panda*.

But Gautam was also surprised at how *The Pioneer* had given away the name of the victim. Wasn't that a serious breach of the press censorship law?

20

An unexpected downpour freshened the Saturday morning. Even though it immobilized all traffic, with rivulets of water swishing across roads and pavements, everyone felt a new fragrance in the atmosphere—the smell of scorched earth drinking in lustily. By noon, however, the rain slowed down to a mere drizzle; then the sun broke through a cluster of grey clouds.

When Gautam reached the Kashana Gate, near the tea-shop, he saw mounted police patrolling the area, their horses' flanks shimmering in the damp sunlight.

It was a buoyant Haseena who appeared at the Gate, a bag in hand, with the kumkum gleaming on her forehead. Immediately Gautam walked over to her, in his dhoti and kurta, with his own bag slung across his shoulder.

They stood a few yards away from the tea-shop, near the traffic lights.

'Have you seen this morning's *Pioneer*?' she asked excitedly.

'You mean the killing on the Ganges?'

'Yes,' she replied. 'Wasn't it our friend from Delhi?'

'Yes.'

'And wasn't he identified by *panda* Bhole?'

'Yes.'

'That unriddles a lot of mystery, doesn't it?'

'Yes.'

Haseena felt somewhat mystified at Gautam's snappy, monosyllabic answers.

A policeman on horseback drew close, looking suspiciously at the couple; then he rode away, assuming they were only lovers.

'The paper says it was a Muslim who did it,' said Haseena.

'A gross fabrication,' said Gautam. 'That's how the press whips up communal passions.'

'Then who might have done it?'

'A Hindu,' Gautam answered. 'And I happen to know it all . . . I witnessed the killing.'

Haseena gazed at him, nonplussed. 'Because *I* did it . . . had to kill the man—myself!' Gautam whispered into her ears.

She heard the words in stark amazement, her eyes dilated, her face flushed. Across the road, a policeman's horse snorted, a tonga-driver lashed his horse into a canter, a military truck rattled past. . .

'How?' she asked, finding it difficult to believe what she'd just heard.

'I got him near the fort—with his own knife,' Gautam's voice was a murmur. 'In sheer self-defence.' He paused. 'You see, he'd come after us. It's a well-knit mafia—the pimp, the *panda* and your kidnappers. But I still feel guilty, somehow.'

As Gautam narrated the incident, Haseena's eyes

sparkled, an expression of relief rippling across her face.

'I love you very much,' she cooed.

'Because I've killed him?'

'No, for profounder reasons,' she breathed. 'And everyone at home now knows about you and me—mother, uncle and Salma.'

'I should have guessed . . . your letter.'

She blushed, looking away, as though she didn't want him to bring it up.

'Why don't you change and come with me to mother?' she said, handing him the bag in which she'd brought him a sherwani and a fez. 'She'd be delighted to hear about the incident from you . . . I'll wipe off my kumkum meanwhile.'

'All right,' he said, walking away to the Gents, near the tea-stall.

As they now walked into Mohalla Kashana, Gautam in his Muslim dress and Haseena without the kumkum, he saw armed police posted at all street corners. There were no blacksmiths fabricating weapons on the pavements. He wondered if the open arsenal had now moved underground. No crowds on the streets too, no vendors anywhere around.

Haseena's mind was still occupied with the killing.

'So the lizard was your saviour,' she said, as she led him into a bylane.

'Yes.'

'Imagine if you hadn't been so nimble-footed.'

'You'd have got your release—your freedom.'

'To do what?'

'To go to Pakistan,' he said, smiling, 'with your family.'

'You're utterly mistaken.'

'Then what would you've done?'

'I'd have sought out your parents, and stayed with them,' she replied. 'One doesn't fall in love twice.'

Haseena wished she'd been in a burkha, covered from head to foot, sheltered from the spoken word, in a discreet veil of privacy.

Gautam felt he could almost hear his heart beating.

They stopped at a corner to let some policemen cross the street.

'I'll try to keep you happy, Haseena.'

'Commitment doesn't look for happiness,' she responded. 'It just wants to belong.'

'At times I wonder if I really deserve you.'

'Love has nothing to do with deserving either,' she said.

Gautam felt impelled to kiss her, right there on the pavement. As he gazed at her face, it seemed so remote, so spiritual.

'In any such relationship,' she resumed, wistfully, 'the body is not the ultimate thing, it's the joy of surrender.'

'Haseena, do you remember all the beautiful things you said in your letter?' Gautam asked.

'Oh, please . . .' she said, embarrassed.

'Of course, sometimes you can say unkind things too.'

She looked at him, surprised.

'What?'

'That bit about virginity.'

'But wouldn't you have liked to marry a virgin?' she asked, a touch of poignancy in her voice.

'Then would you have liked to marry a divorcee?' he countered.

When they stepped into the house, they saw Begum Rahim on her knees, praying—her head covered by a thin veil, her hands raised, palms upwards. Sheikh Ahmed rose from his cane chair as he saw them enter, but he didn't say anything lest he disturb his sister in her namaz. It was only after a few minutes that Haseena's mother opened her eyes.

'What's happened?' she asked, looking surprised. 'You're back so soon—both.' Then, turning to Gautam, 'You see, I pray each time Haseena goes out—for her safety, for peace . . . I hear there'll soon be a raid on our mohalla.'

'Why should you worry?' said Gautam. 'Wouldn't your prayers be enough protection against any danger? And, then, the authorities now mean business.'

'I'm not so sure,' she replied.'They've been doling out assurances all these days. Words, words. . .'

'Look, ammijan,' Haseena interjected, 'Gautam's here with some good news for you.'

'What?'

'The man killed on the river was my abductor.'

'Oh, let Allah be praised!' Begum Rahim exclaimed.

'And guess who killed him?' Haseena asked.

'Who?'

'Gautam!' Haseena exclaimed exultantly. 'Yes, he did it.'

Begum Rahim's dazed eyes probed Gautam's face.

Sheikh Ahmed and Salma also stared at him, stunned.

'It seems he'd come after us,' said Gautam, 'all the way from Delhi. He ambushed me near the fort. So I had no choice but to . . .'

'Oh Allah!' Begum Rahim raised her hands prayerfully, out of joy and gratitude.

'Maybe I was able to defend myself because of your blessings, your prayers,' said Gautam sombrely.

There was a brief silence.

'May I ask a boon of you, ammijan?' asked Gautam.

Haseena's mother felt touched to be again addressed as ammijan.

'Allah alone is the giver of boons, my dear,' she answered.

'But this one is for you to give.'

'What's it?'

'I want to marry Haseena,' he almost stuttered, tense and anxious. 'I need your blessings.'

There was no immediate response from Haseena's mother, who was now lost in some deep thought. While Salma kept staring at Gautam, Sheikh Ahmed broke in: 'But what about the different worlds? In our shariat, you'll have to receive the Kalma Sharif, accept Islam, before any such marriage could be solemnized.'

'I'll do it, gladly.'

As Gautam spoke these words, his eyes settled on the kalma inscribed in gilded letters on the plaque, above the mantelpiece. Then he turned to Haseena, whose face was glowing like a candle in a crystal vase.

His answer had made everyone speechless; a hush descended upon the room.

'But what about your parents? Will they accept your conversion?' asked Sheikh Ahmed, looking sceptical.

'Nobody else matters.'

'Look Ahmed,' Haseena's mother interjected. 'There's nothing more to say. If it's God's will, let it be.'

'Thank you ammijan,' said Gautam. 'God bless you!'

'There's, however, one snag, my son,' Begum Rahim

said. 'As you know already, we've decided to migrate to Pakistan—and that decision is absolute, irrevocable.' She paused for a moment, then resumed: 'I can't let Salma be whisked away next. You can't take charge of the entire family when there are abductors lurking everywhere. So, it's time to go—to another country, I know, not ours. Leaving Allahabad would be the greatest wrench. But there's no alternative. Ahmed will, however, stay back for a while to manage a few things—he'll join us later.'

'I understand,' said Gautam.

'So it's for Haseena to decide,' said Begum Rahim; then turning to her: 'Do you also want. . .' she broke off, as if not knowing how to round it off.

'Yes, ammijan.'

'Then God bless you both.'

'Thank you,' Gautam said. Then after a brief pause, he added: 'Since I'd planned to complete my assignment before returning to Delhi tomorrow, may I take Haseena with me this afternoon as well?' That, as you know, was our programme today.'

'Isn't she yours now, my son, to take care of?' Haseena's mother asked.

But as Gautam stood up to leave, Haseena's mother said, 'I wonder if you could help us with our immigration papers. We don't know anybody in Delhi.'

'Surely, ammijan. I should be able to get it done.'

As they both returned to the traffic lights near the tea-shop, Gautam went into the rest room to change into dhoti and kurta, while Haseena put on her kumkum.

Then they stood on the pavement, waiting for some tonga or taxi to take them downtown. Gautam felt that before returning to Delhi, he should really go around the city to be able to report to his paper authentically.

A taxi pulled up beside them on the road, and a face peered out of the rear window.

'Hi, could you help us, please?' the man asked. 'We want to see Nehru House, but our cabby doesn't seem to understand us.'

It was an American couple, Gautam guessed, out sightseeing. Americans, he knew, were particularly welcome anywhere in the country for their warm friendliness and their dollars—in spite of the communal turmoil.

'You mean his birthplace?' Gautam asked, drawing close to the taxi.

'Yeah,' the American tourist replied, getting off, a heavy camera slung across his shoulders, a copy of the Blue Guide in hand, while his wife kept sitting inside.

'Well, the place is really known as Anand Bhavan,' said Gautam, 'not Nehru House.'

Immediately, the taxi-driver nodded his head as though the riddle had been solved.

'Thanks a lot,' said the man, his freckled face glowing in the sun. 'Can we give you a ride?'

'In fact, we are going the same way,' Gautam answered. 'We'd be grateful.'

'Most welcome,' said the man. 'Come on in . . . Maybe you could also tell us what else to see in town. There's, I understand, also the sacred cave under the Kali Satum Temple?'

'Yes, the driver should know that one too,' Gautam said, beckoning Haseena to sit in the rear, while he sat in front with the driver.

'We're Americans,' the man said. 'This is my wife, Alice, and I'm Jim Clarke. Call me just Jim.'

'How do you do?' said Gautam, looking back; then he added, 'this is my fiancée, Haseena, and I'm Gautam Mehta. Call me Gautam.'

'Gautam, isn't she real pretty?' said Alice.

'Well, she's all right for me,' Gautam replied, darting a furtive glance at Haseena.

'Look at him,' Alice said, turning to her husband, 'as if he doesn't know what he's got there. A fancy doll, that's what she is.'

Haseena flushed. There was a brief pause.

'Excuse me, are you Hindus?' Alice asked.

Obviously, the American couple had not guessed anything from their names; otherwise, Gautam thought, they should have sensed the communal mix-up.

'I'm a Hindu,' Gautam said, thinking it unnecessary to bring in his conversion to Christianity. 'But my fiancée is a Muslim.'

'But is it at all possible?' Jim asked, utterly surprised.

'Not ordinarily,' Gautam replied, seeing that even these foreigners had understood the communal situation in India.

'But what's wrong if you're in love?' said Alice.

'Of course,' said Jim. 'It's just that the two communities are at war with each other, aren't they?'

'Yes,' interjected Haseena. 'But should religion be a barrier?'

'No,' replied Jim, impressed with the sudden sharp remark of the young Indian woman. 'What a shame we kill each other in the name of God!'

'That happens when our religion is just a political

posture,' said Haseena, 'not a matter of conviction.'

'There you are,' said Alice; then looking at her husband: 'Isn't Gautam lucky to have someone like her? Beauty and mind!'

Haseena turned crimson.

'Eh, Jim, why don't you tell them about the *panda* we met on the river this morning?' said Alice.

'Oh that guy? . . . He sure was something, Jesus.' He paused. 'What was his name, honey?' he turned to his wife.

'Panda Bhole,' she answered.

At the mention of the name, Gautam and Haseena sat up in their seats, startled.

'You know,' Jim resumed, 'he was a real leviathan. We took several pictures of him. He just kept jabbering away in his native tongue, so our guide couldn't give us all that he said. But I remember his telling us how he'd met a Muslim couple masquerading as Hindu honeymooners. He was going on as if he was after them. What kind of religious man was he?'

He stopped only when the taxi braked in front of a buffalo, straying across the street, its owner just ambling behind the animal. The taxi was now racing through the eastern sector of the town.

'Gautam, how can one tell a Hindu from a Muslim?' Jim asked.

'They look about the same,' Gautam answered, 'specially Hindu and Muslim women in saris, except that a Muslim woman doesn't put on the kumkum—a dot on the forehead. Sherwani, a knee-length, tight-fitting jacket, and a fez is the dress for a Muslim man, while a Hindu ordinarily wears a dhoti and kurta.'

'Like what you are wearing?' asked Alice.

'Yes.'

'Then why has Haseena put on that dot?' asked Alice, taking a side-glance at her.

'Since we have to move about in a predominantly Hindu city,' replied Gautam. 'It's a shame. . .'

'Now we understand,' said Alice. 'You know, we love India in spite of the little mess you are in these days.'

'It's a lot of mess,' said Gautam. 'I do hope it'll be cleaned up soon.'

'But whatever the problems,' said Jim, 'India is now a free country. You always had our sympathies, you know.'

'Every Indian knows that,' said Gautam. 'You were with us all the way.'

Alice broke into a broad smile, gratified.

'India has a glorious future,' said Jim.

'But a bleak present,' Gautam quipped. 'First, we must have peace before we can settle down to our freedom.'

'That's it,' said Jim. 'Heard about our Statue of Liberty?'

'Of course.'

'Then you know how we feel about freedom,' said Alice.

The taxi pulled up in front of a two-storey palatial building, glistening under a lingum-shaped dome, looking like an observatory—a spacious lawn in front, guava and mango trees on either side.

'I guess, you may have already seen the place,' said Jim, 'but we'd be delighted if you could stay with us a little longer. We could then all go somewhere and have tea or something.'

Haseena, who was feeling impatient to be alone with Gautam, said, 'We'd have loved to stay with you but, unfortunately, we have to go somewhere.'

'That's fine,' said Alice. 'But we hope we'll meet again.'

'Yes, come and visit with us,' said Jim, 'in Cleveland, Ohio—our home town.'

'Maybe we will, some day,' said Gautam.

Instantly, Jim took out his wallet from his hip pocket. As he unzipped it, there flashed out several plastic folds showing his identity card, his driving licence—and some snaps. Taking out the photographs, he said: 'These are our kids—five of them. Three daughters, two sons. Pam, Karen, Mary, Jack and Chris . . . But isn't that kind of unbalanced? I always ask Alice to produce one more son so that the family may be evenly paired.'

They both laughed.

'Aren't they charming?' Gautam said, looking at the snaps. Gautam and Haseena got off at the next traffic light, saying goodbye to the American tourists.

A quick tour of the city showed Gautam the enormity of communal tension. In spite of the police patrolling all parts of the city, it seemed as though the two communities, sworn to eternal enmity, were primed for another clash, mostly over Pannalal's killing. How very ironical, Gautam thought, that while he strongly believed in communal harmony, tolerance and peace, he had himself become the cause of tension in the city.

As he brought Haseena back to the Kashana Gate, he became sullen. This was the moment of parting.

'I must leave for Delhi tomorrow,' he said, his voice heavy, 'to report to duty on Monday.'

'I know,' Haseena also sounded low.

'But I'll be back,' said Gautam, 'as soon as I am able to do something about the immigration papers for Salma and ammijan.'

'That may take quite a while, I'm afraid.'

'Perhaps Berry could be of some help if he's got to know the police commissioner through an English friend of ours.'

'That should certainly expedite matters.'

'I propose to escort ammijan and Salma personally to Wagah, near Amritsar.'

'Is that the international border between India and Pakistan?'

'Yes.'

'Haven't you taken too much upon yourself?' Haseena said, looking at him ardently.

'If I have your love, I could walk through fire,' he said.

That night he sat up, till early morning, to finish the report he'd been commissioned to do for his paper.

21

It was a blitzkrieg, planned and executed with the uncanny precision of a hyena. Straight from Bob's party, William Thornton first drove off to Asaf Ali Road to ensure that the arson in the cinema hall wouldn't lead to rioting, then to his control room. Hurriedly, he summoned all his aides and ordered a surprise raid on the brothel behind Neel Kamal, exactly at 11:45, the following night. He directed that half an hour before the raid, all entrances and exits within a mile of the restaurant should be sealed off. A crack party of armed policemen, led by himself, would then comb all the lanes around Neel Kamal to locate the brothel!

That evening, the weather took a sharp turn. A little before sunset, the sky became overcast with clouds; then at about half past ten, a heavy shower drove away almost all pedestrians from Faiz Bazaar and its bylanes. Even the tobacconist near Neel Kamal, who ordinarily kept his stall open till midnight, pulled down the shutters and went home. The entire place now wore a weird look.

Precisely at 11:15, a fleet of police jeeps zoomed in from two opposite directions, from Delhi Gate and

Victoria Zenana Hospital. Batches of policemen jumped off their jeeps, taking positions at the mouth of each lane. Surprised by this unusual operation, the manager of Neel Kamal asked one of the policemen: 'Is there a riot or arson anywhere around?'

'I don't know,' replied the policeman. 'Will you remain inside your restaurant for the next three hours? These are our orders.'

The manager went inside his restaurant, utterly confounded.

Then a jeep, with a superintendent of police at the steering wheel and the police commissioner seated beside him, penetrated a lane along the Diamond Cinema, followed by a dozen armed policemen on foot. But a few yards further down the lane, the jeep had to be abandoned because the passage was too narrow. The commissioner now led his party on foot, wedging deeper into the area. The snorting of the jeep had, however, already awakened most of the residents who began to look out of their windows, astounded and terrified.

As an old bearded man, in a soiled sherwani, emerged from a dilapidated room, shuffling towards the street urinal, the superintendent of police ordered him to stop.

'Who are you?'

'I live over there, sir,' the man replied, pointing towards his room across the lane. He felt almost paralysed to see armed policemen prowling all around.

'With your family?'

'Alone, sir,' came the tremulous reply.

At this point, William Thornton himself stepped forward. The appearance of someone, looking like an

Englishman, decorated with epaulettes and medals, scared him out of his wits.

'There is a brothel around here, old man . . . Where's it?' The commissioner asked him in Anglicized Hindustani.

'I don't know, sir,' the man stuttered.

Poking him in the ribs with the butt of his revolver, the superintendent of police shouted: 'Don't waste our time!'

The pressure of urine deepening in his bladder, and fear gripping his heart, the old man lost his nerve. Of course, he knew where the brothel was, but he was also aware that a word from him would endanger his life. The mafia would wipe him out forthwith. So he stood there, mute and bewildered.

The superintendent of police now grabbed him by the beard and punched him hard in the stomach. The old man doubled up, and began to cry.

'You want another?' the superintendent asked, pulling hard at his beard.

'They'll kill me, sir,' stuttered the man, looking beseechingly at the commissioner.

'Who're they?' asked William Thornton.

'Pannalal, Suleiman Ghani and the others.'

The first name rang a bell in Thornton's mind. Wasn't this the name his control room had picked up in the wireless message from Allahabad? The papers had put him out as 'a Hindu pilgrim from Delhi'. Although Pannalal was a common Hindu name, the commissioner decided to link it up with the killing on the Ganges—as a strategy.

'Pannalal is already dead,' said the commissioner. 'Killed in Allahabad. Didn't you read about it in the papers?'

The old ignoramus merely blinked like an idiot, then

replied: 'There'll still be Suleiman Ghani, sir—he'll get me.'

'He's been arrested,' said the commissioner. 'So why are you afraid?'

'I can only point out the house from here, sir,' he replied, his voice a mute whisper.

'That should be all right,' said the commissioner. 'You needn't be fearful of anybody now. We'll guarantee you full protection. So tell us—quick.'

But as the old man pointed his finger towards a large mansion further down the lane, the commissioner saw someone with a gun leap across its roof to the adjoining terrace. Immediately, he ordered a sniper from his party to shoot him down. As the bullet got the man on the housetop, a shriek slashed the air, followed by the sound of a body falling down.

'Well done!' said the commissioner, turning to the sniper.

'But how could Ghani be arrested, sir?' the old man asked, looking distrustfully at the commissioner. 'That man just shot down was he.'

Merely grinning, the commissioner ordered his men to cordon off the brothel. Its front door was then rammed open, and the party trooped in. Within a few minutes, Ghani was captured, his leg bleeding profusely. He was carried away in a police jeep.

By now all the lights in the lane had been switched on, and stunned faces peered out of the windows and balconies. But nobody dared come out into the lane even though it was evident that the brothel had been raided.

As William Thornton and his men entered the building, they were shocked to witness a gruesome spectacle. A woman, in her mid-forties, with a bottle of kerosene oil in her right hand, was forcing a young girl into a blazing fire in the courtyard. But each time she caught hold of her, the other girls pulled her out and instead tried to shove the woman herself into the fire.

'Take that woman into custody,' the commissioner ordered a policeman.

She was dragged out of the house and whisked away in a jeep.

For a few minutes, all the young girls, Hindu or Muslim, couldn't believe they'd been rescued. They looked about dazed; then a full-throated cheer broke through: 'Shukriya! Thank you, sir!'

Like a flock of caged birds, suddenly set free, they fluttered about the courtyard, happy and excited.

'You are our saviour, sir!' exclaimed the tall girl who'd narrowly missed getting pushed into the fire. 'A few minutes more and she'd have done us all to ashes.'

'Nobody will harm you now,' assured the commissioner. 'It's all over. You're free.'

'Are we?' said the tall girl, still incredulous.

'Yes, you are—free to go back to your homes. We'll arrange everything for you.'

Suddenly, the tall girl's brow darkened.

'But Pannalal's still at large,' she said. 'He'll hound us down somehow. He has contacts everywhere.'

'Pannalal?' the commissioner pondered as he repeated the name. 'Where's he?'

'We don't know,' replied another girl. 'But I did overhear the other day about his secret visit to Allahabad. I told my friends he must have gone after Haseena, a girl who'd escaped from here.'

'Haseena?'

'Yes, sir. She'd been abducted from there.'

'So Pannalal was in Allahabad on Friday.' The commissioner was turning over something in his mind, making connections.

'Possibly.'

'Then he's gone,' said the commissioner. 'He was the man stabbed to death there last Friday. Didn't you read your Saturday paper?'

'No papers here, sir. It's a dungeon.'

But all the girls now looked happy and relieved.

'What's your name?' the commissioner asked the tall girl.

'Lakshmi, sir.'

'Haseena and Lakshmi!' the commissioner intoned; then, turning to the superintendent of police, he observed: 'Here's a real intercommunal home, with Pannalal and Suleiman Ghani as its heads.'

The superintendent's response was a subdued smile.

'Where're you from, Lakshmi?' the commissioner asked.

'Multan—West Pakistan. I lost my entire family in the riots there. I was captured by some gang, then passed on to Pannalal.'

'Do you have any relatives in India?'

'An uncle in Bombay.'

'We'll send you there,' said the commissioner; then turning to the other girls, he assured them: 'You'll all be back home soon.' After a pause, he asked Lakshmi: 'Tell me, how were these devils operating?'

Beckoning the commissioner and his men to follow her, she took them to a row of small dingy rooms, encircling the central courtyard. Each room, damp and windowless, had a bamboo cot, an earthen pitcher and some utensils. On the bare wet floors crawled cockroaches, while the roofs and walls threatened to cave in any time.

'Death cells!' muttered the commissioner, looking into one of the rooms.

'Death was the penalty,' said Lakshmi, 'for anyone trying to escape. Death by fire! You've already seen how the woman wanted to kill me for eavesdropping.'

Lakshmi then led the party to a room on the first floor, which was furnished like an office. On the shelves were arranged ledgers and files, while in a corner stood a steel vault.

'There,' said Lakshmi, pointing to the vault, 'should be wads of currency notes. We were asked to bring in foreign currency preferably, from the customers from abroad—Americans, Europeans, the Sheikhs from the Middle East. . .'

'Looks like they also operated as racketeers in foreign exchange,' said the commissioner; then turning to the superintendent of police, he said: 'Will you please have everything in this vault sealed for subsequent investigation?'

'Yes, sir.'

William Thornton now realized that he'd busted a multifaceted racket—prostitution, murder, violation of foreign exchange and what not. He must ask Bob, he told himself, to thank his Indian friend, Birendra Dhawan, for putting him on to it.

'And what about Neel Kamal?' the commissioner asked Lakshmi. 'Did these pimps have any links with that restaurant?'

'Surely,' she replied. 'There was some dubious connection, sir. Sort of partnership. For one thing, its manager often came here to have drinks with Pannalal and Ghani. Also, we all knew that Pannalal picked up most of his customers from Neel Kamal.'

'I see . . . were you allowed to go out with your customers?'

'Never. Only as far as the Bridge Hotel.'

'Hmm . . .'

As the party was about to come out of the building, Lakshmi asked the commissioner if he'd also like to have a look at 'a special room', near the front door. He nodded his head in affirmation.

This room was luxuriously furnished, in glaring contrast with the sordid, dismal cells he'd just seen. There were two cushioned divans, one rocking chair padded with velvet, an improvised bar with a large variety of liquors—Indian and foreign. On a side-table lay a half-filled glass, with a bottle of Scotch near it. The commissioner wondered if Ghani was having his midnight swig when he was nabbed. On the walls hung large photographs of popular film stars.

'This is surely something exclusive,' said the commissioner.

'This is where Pannalal and Ghani entertained their special guests to midnight orgies.'

'I can't understand,' the commissioner said, rather sharply, 'why didn't you use any of your customers to contact the police?'

'Would that have helped?'

'What do you mean?'

'The truth is that even the policemen were in league with the pimps.'

The commissioner felt stung; then he turned around to the superintendent and asked: 'Will you look into the credentials of all the policemen posted around Neel Kamal, and the Bridge? This is scandalous. How can we inspire confidence in the public when we are to blame ourselves?'

'But these policemen, sir,' the superintendent replied, 'are frequently transferred from one station to another. I think it'll be a futile exercise.'

'You're right,' said the commissioner. 'The entire set-up is rotten to the core.'

The commissioner then ordered his policemen to help the girls pack up, and then escort them to the Parliament Police Station. Walking up the lane, at the head of his party, he saw the old man still standing near the urinal.

'Thank you, Maulana sahib,' said the commissioner, 'for all your help. Don't worry at all. In a day or two, we're going to clean up the entire area. Just telephone my control room if you sense any danger.'

The old man felt deeply touched by the commissioner's solicitude.

As the commissioner and the superintendent left, the policemen grumbled among themselves over Lakshmi's disclosure about the collusion between the pimps and the police. They were worried lest some of their colleagues should be identified and sacked. Since William Thornton himself had led the raid, they knew he wouldn't spare anyone found guilty.

Moreover, the tantalizing sight of a bevy of young and beautiful girls frustrated them utterly. They felt like small children in a candy store, who have been forbidden to touch anything.

Next morning, all the papers carried a detailed report of the raid, based on 'eyewitnesses' accounts'—also of the brutal murder of an old Muslim who'd acted as an informer to the commissioner. On his gagged mouth was pasted a piece of paper which said: 'For talking too much!'

It was rumoured that he'd been killed by one of the policemen on duty, around Neel Kamal.

22

Gautam's train brought him to Delhi early Monday morning. He felt excited to read in the papers about the police raid on the brothel. Since Berry, he thought, might know more about it, he decided to meet him before moving on to Anand Parbat. When he reached Berry's, he saw him having his coffee, on the front lawn, a pile of newspapers scattered all around him.

'Welcome home!' exclaimed Berry, beckoning Gautam to a side-chair. 'Are you coming directly from the station?'

'Yes.'

'Read the morning papers?'

'The raid on the brothel?'

'Then you know it all,' said Berry. 'Isn't that great?'

'So the den's cleaned up.'

'But who put Thornton sahib on to it?' asked Berry, winking. 'I met him at Bob's party.'

'I should have guessed.'

'But first let me get you some breakfast,' said Berry.

As Berry called Shyama, she breezed in, again dressed in one of Sonali's saris.

'Some coffee and toast for Mehta sahib, please,' Berry asked Shyama.

'Yes, sir.'

'Oh dear,' Gautam said, seeing the maidservant walk away, swaying her hips, 'that "sirring!"—very impressive indeed.' He smiled. 'But where's Sonali? Away at her aunt's?'

'This time I really don't know where she's gone,' Berry answered. 'Just packed up yesterday afternoon and vanished.'

'Another divorce in the offing?'

'I don't know . . . Maybe you should teach me also some Bible to get around Father Jones,' Berry laughed. 'Second time's always a lot easier.'

'Has it come to this?'

'Well, we had a little wrangle,' Berry said, nonchalantly. 'You know, I couldn't have taken her to Bob's party.'

'I understand.'

'The great pity is that she'd be back soon.'

'Oh, you callous thing.'

'No, I've already started missing her.'

'That too I can understand.'

As Shyama brought in the breakfast tray, Gautam began to drink his coffee.

'Look,' said Berry, 'I've some great news for you.'

'What?'

'Mohinder and Sarita got married, the day before yesterday.'

'Wonderful!' exclaimed Gautam, putting down his cup of coffee.

'I got the news from Shyama, who picked it up from Purnima, who got it from Padamnath Trivedi—and he should know all the news of the world.'

'Of course,' Gautam said, still looking surprised. 'What intrigues me most is why she plunged into marriage so soon.'

'I can guess the reasons.'

'What?'

'It seems the man who jeeped you down to the station after your escape from the Bridge talked about your running away with a beautiful girl. The word reached Mohinder, then obviously Sarita . . . Provoked, she must have hustled Mohinder into it. Poor man!'

'Well, he asked for it,' said Gautam. 'But how did Trivedi pick up the press gossip?'

'Maybe he knows one of your reporters.'

'Interesting . . . Well, I should then thank Bala for all his help, and for giving us the ride.'

'Sure, you owe it all to him,' said Berry. 'You know, it's only when an ex-wife remarries that she gets off your back. Otherwise, she's always on the scent—spying, scandalmongering, weaving her little cocoon of malice and revenge.'

'So now I should feel free to do anything.'

'What?'

'Marry Haseena,' said Gautam. 'Not on the rebound, though.'

'Has it gone that far?' Berry said, a little surprised.

'Why not? . . . I've fallen in love with her.'

'Then I couldn't tell your old man everything,' said Berry.

'Did he see you?'

'Well, he came here the other day to ask about you. He looked very worried. You should have dropped him a word from Allahabad. But I imagine you were in bed with her all the time.'

'Don't be funny. Tell me. . .'

'I did let him know something about you and Haseena.'

'What did he say?' Gautam's gaze now settled on Berry's face.

'He just listened,' Berry answered. 'A marvellous man! I wish I had a father like yours.'

'I should thank you for clearing the decks for me,' Gautam said; then, after a pause, he added: 'Look, I'll need your help again . . . How close did you get to the commissioner at Bob's party?'

'I can't say. But there's always Bob.'

'All right, let me explain,' said Gautam. 'Haseena's mother and her sister have decided to migrate to Pakistan. You know there's no security for Muslims in Allahabad, or anywhere in India.'

'But how does the commissioner come into this?'

'I'll need some police escort from Delhi to Amritsar. Also some influence to get the immigration papers for them.'

'That's a tall order,' said Berry. 'But I'll do my best, lover boy,' he added.

'Thank you.'

'And Mrs Haseena Mehta will, of course, stay back,' Berry smiled.

'Naturally.'

Till now, Gautam had deliberately held back his

encounter with Pannalal—how he'd killed him. He wanted to bring it up as dramatically as possible.

'You may have also read about the killing of a Hindu pilgrim in Allahabad,' Gautam said.

'Of course. I had it straight from the commissioner, at Bob's party. Even before the press flashed it the next morning.'

'Well, it was our friend, the pimp.'

'Pannalal?' Berry asked, quite surprised. 'If I remember correctly, it was a Muslim who killed him. That's what the press reported—of course, in the usual journalistic euphemism, "killed by a member of the minority community".'

'Nonsense,' Gautam said. 'I did it—I got him with his own knife, but out of sheer self-defence.' A pause. He then added: 'Hadn't you got him stripped on the platform? So he came after us . . .'

Berry craned his neck forward to take a close look at Gautams' face.

'Are you fantasizing?' he said, sceptically. 'How could a spineless, non-violent creature like you kill a tough , sly guy like Pannalal?'

Then, as Gautam narrated the entire incident, Berry felt as though he was listening to an incredible tale.

'But now a greater ordeal awaits me,' Gautam said. 'Facing my parents.'

'You'll come through.'

'I don't know,' Gautam mumbled, standing up to leave. 'My old man must be wondering why I'm fooling around with Christians and Muslims.'

By the time Gautam got to Anand Parbat, it was about eleven. Answering the door, his mother flashed a cold, stern look at him. After the divorce, she'd started negotiating her son's second marriage; in fact, she already had in mind a couple of girls, beautiful and educated.

Then Berry blew up the bombshell.

'Running away from me, mother?' Gautam held her back by the hand.

'What's left for me to look forward to?'

'I know you're very angry with me . . . But then you don't know enough.'

'Maybe I know too much,' she flared up, and walked away.

It would be futile arguing with her now, Gautam thought. She was obviously worked up. His father, who was reading something in his room, emerged on hearing Gautam's voice.

'It was a long stay, Gautam,' he said.

'Yes, father. I'm sorry.'

'Got your assignment done?'

'I've brought it along. I'll hand it in tomorrow, though I should have done it today.'

They were just hedging around, Gautam knew. But, thank God, his father didn't look tense like his mother.

'I met Berry the other day,' his father said, in a heavy voice.

'Yes, he's told me.'

'When?'

'I stopped by at Berry's house for a few minutes.'

'Oh, I see.'

There was a brief pause.

'Are you angry with me, Dad?'

'No.'

'I need your blessings.'

'You already have them,' said Shyamlal, tenderly. 'And don't you worry about your mother. She'll come around. Give her a little time.'

'Thank you very much,' Gautam said, intensely moved by his father's ready approval.

Gautam's eyes fell upon a large leather-bound book whose green title caught his attention—The Koran. He picked it up from his father's table, fascinated by the picture on the jacket—an angelic reader, bending over an open page, on which the sunbeams descended from the sky.

'Yes,' Gautam's father said, asking him to sit in a chair close by. 'I've been reading this for the past couple of days.'

'I understand . . .' Gautam wondered if his father was still inwardly troubled about something.

'You know,' said Shyamlal, 'I should thank you for bringing me to this great book.' Then, taking it from Gautam's hand, he opened it on a page underscored in red. 'Will you read out this bit—aloud?'

The passage was titled 'The Laws', from one of the sermons given by the Prophet:

All human beings are created as a family
A single community
Then God sends His Prophets
Bearers of glad tidings,
Who guide those who believe in Him
And punish the evil.

As soon as he finished reading, his father asked: 'Now isn't that what Lord Krishna also says in the Bhagavadgita? 'Whenever righteousness declines and evil prospers, I assume a visible shape and move as man with man, guiding the virtuous, punishing the wicked . . .' Don't you have here two Prophets saying the same thing?'

'Yes, father.'

'And yet there's so much hatred between Hindus and Muslims.'

'Then wasn't Prophet Mohammad,' remarked Gautam, 'also an avatar?'

'Most certainly,' replied his father. 'Like Jesus, the Buddha, Guru Nanak and even Swami Dayanand. Didn't you notice in this passage from the Koran that God sends, from time to time, His bearers of glad tidings? There, you have a clear enunciation of a sort of universal prophethood that embraces all religions—Hinduism, Christianity and Islam.'

Gautam now sensed how his father had worked himself into this rhetoric. Had he really come around to this realization, or was he merely rationalizing his son's love for a Muslim girl?

Outside the window, some urchins were chasing a mad man who'd stripped himself stark naked.

'I played chess with God last night,' the lunatic was squealing away, 'and I beat him—hands down. Poor thing! When he grinned, I noticed that he'd several abscessed teeth. Bleeding gums too! And they still call him God Almighty.'

'How much did he lose to you?' asked one of the urchins.

'A tenner! But I let him go. You know, he is also a pauper like me.'

The man then broke into a peal of laughter.

The noise brought Gautam's mother to the window. Looking at her husband and son, she said: 'I see madness everywhere, even inside this house. There's just one lunatic out there but there're two right in here.'

'Don't be so nasty, Radha,' Shamlal cut in. 'Why don't you let us talk in peace?'

She shuffled away, grumbling. 'All right, why don't you settle everything between the two of you?'

'Don't be upset, Gautam,' said his father, 'she'll be all right.' He paused. 'I just want to ask you something . . . How far have you gone with this Muslim girl?'

'I want to marry her, father.'

A brief silence.

'Will it be a Muslim wedding?' Shamlal asked.

'Yes.'

'I don't mind.'

'Thank you, father.'

'When?'

'Any time—in Allahabad . . .'

'I see,' Shamlal muttered. 'Then go ahead, my son.'

'Thank you,' Gautam said. A pause. 'Her mother and sister want to migrate to Pakistan. They see no future in India. And I have offered to escort them up to Amritsar.'

'I understand,' said his father. 'But wouldn't that be a very dangerous undertaking?' There was a tremor in his voice as though something had disturbed his equanimity.

'Someone will have to do it for them . . . Perhaps Berry could help. He knows the police commissioner.'

'Then it's all settled.'

'You've been more than a friend to me.'

'Shouldn't that be the only relationship between father and son?' Shamlal said.

Using William Thornton's influence with the Pakistan High Commission, Berry was able to get the immigration papers processed expeditiously. The police commissioner also offered to arrange for an armed police escort for Berry's friends for their train journey from Delhi to Amritsar. Wasn't Thornton grateful to Berry for his tip in busting the brothel?

The next morning, Gautam wrote a detailed letter to Haseena, informing her that he had secured his parents' approval—and that he had also got the immigration papers for her mother and Salma. But he added that he might have to stay back in Delhi for about a fortnight to attend to his official duties before he could apply for leave.

23

'I believe Mahatma Gandhi is essentially a radical socialist,' said the editor of *The Challenge*. The creaking of the ceiling fan partly drowned his voice.

'But what about his religious eclecticism?' Gautam responded, inwardly anxious to know what his editor had to say about his article on communal harmony.

'That was only a camouflage,' the editor replied, his eyes flashing under his thick brows, which almost joined across his nose bridge.

In spite of his stern appearance, Gautam had always liked his boss for his pliant willingness to be challenged. In fact, everyone on the staff knew that the more you disagreed with him, the more he admired you.

'But hasn't he written a very perceptive treatise on the Gita?'

'There too,' the editor said, 'he is basically concerned with the concept of social justice . . . Didn't he say only the other day that the lowliest of our people are the true salt of the Indian nation?' He paused. Then, he added: 'Incidentally, haven't you also stressed the point that the poor man, whether Hindu, Muslim or Christian, is indifferent to communal politics? He just wants his bread and shelter.' Then, nodding his head in affirmation, he added, 'That was well said.'

'Thank you very much,' Gautam said, feeling gratified.

He then wondered if his editor had heard about his conversion to Christianity—also about Mohinder's marriage to Sarita. But, surely, he couldn't have known anything about his love for a Muslim girl. There, even his radical socialism would have perhaps failed him, for wasn't he at heart a committed Hindu?

'My only quarrel with your article is,' the editor said, looking directly at Gautam, 'that it has a palpable religious slant . . . You seem to be moving towards Gandhi, as you understand him—towards a sort of universal religion.'

'Maybe,' Gautam said, 'because I can't divorce the Mahatma's political views from his deeper awareness of religion as a force that should bring man closer to man.'

'Well,' the editor's voice now rose above the ceiling fan's loud whirring, 'you still have to know the man more closely to see how subtly his mind operates . . . Maybe, you'd like to follow up your article with something on Gandhi's prayer meetings at the Birla House.'

'I should love to . . .'

'You may then see,' the editor was back on his track, 'that by juxtaposing all religions, he is, in fact, trying to neutralize any kind of religious commitment into his own brand of socialism—a social order cutting across caste, creed and colour. And since our nation, fed for centuries on these prejudices, is not yet ready for his Utopia, he may get hurt one of these days.'

'He's certainly far ahead of our times.'

'Yes,' the editor concurred. 'Let's have your comments on the prayer meetings which, I understand, are attracting large crowds.'

'I should find this assignment very exciting.'

'In that case,' said the editor, 'I'll ask Mohinder to drop these meetings and cover only the local events.'

The mere mention of this name stung Gautam. Was the editor discreetly trying to keep them apart, like a referee coming in between two incensed boxers? Gautam now realized the impossibility of continuing with his job at *The Challenge* in spite of his liking for the editor. How long could he avoid running into Mohinder, now his former wife's husband?

But, for the time being, he was caught up with the idea of covering the Mahatma's evening prayer meetings. Prayers, sacred or profane, had begun to fascinate him—Father Jones's for his long happiness, Begum Rahim's for her deceased husband and Panda Bhole's mercenary mumbojumbo at the Triveni . . .

When Gautam announced his assignment to his father, Shamlal looked interested.

'You never take me along anywhere,' he said. 'You cut me out of your baptism . . . What kind of friendship is this?'

Gautam responded with a broad smile.

'Of course, Dad, you're most welcome,' he said, 'though I should caution you that it wouldn't be anything like your Sunday havan at the Arya Samaj temple. And I'll be on duty, awfully busy.'

'I know all this,' said Shamlal. 'But don't forget his prayer meetings are not for journalists only.'

But just as Gautam got himself ready for the prayer

meeting, the Mahatma announced his fast unto death. When the Government of India, under direction from Gandhi, ordered the police to evict, from all mosques, the Hindu refugees who'd started using them as their halls of residence, there were angry protests. Incited by the Hindu fanatics, the refugees burst into another round of communal frenzy. This provoked Gandhi into taking this desperate step.

His fast worked as a miracle: peace committees, headed by senior leaders of both warring communities, mushroomed overnight. He took a glass of orange juice to break his fast only after he'd been assured of peace by both Hindus and Muslims.

A week later, Gandhi announced the resumption of his prayer meetings at the Birla House, a palatial building owned by an affluent Hindu philanthropist, who always hosted Gandhi during his stay in the capital.

As Gautam and his father arrived at the Birla House, an hour ahead of time, they noticed a group of people already gathered on the lawn facing a wooden platform. While Shamlal entered into conversation with some bystanders, mostly Punjabis, Gautam looked about, taking mental notes of the place.

The prayer ground stood some distance away from the Birla House, which was raised in red sandstone. In between lay a rose garden on one side, and a number of petunia beds on the other. The gardener seemed to have tended the flower beds with scrupulous care. A few yards away, to the left of the prayer platform, stood a small family temple.

Precisely at five, Gandhi emerged from the Birla House,

and started walking towards the prayer ground, his hands resting gently on the shoulders of two young ladies. Immediately, the crowd rose in respect, a hush descending all over the place. Then everyone sat down quietly, after the Mahatma took his seat on the platform.

Then began the prayers. The first was a chant from a Buddhist scripture, the second a few verses from the Gita, the third a Parsi hymn, followed by Cardinal Newman's 'Lead, Kindly Light'. But as someone began to recite from the Koran, Gautam's father exchanged an omniscient look with his son. The Mahatma had chosen precisely the same verses from the Koran:

All human beings are created as a family
A single community . . .

The entire sequence of prayers then concluded with a rhythmical hand-clapping and head-swaying to the Ramdhun, the choral part of the evening's programme:

Called by diverse names
Bhagwan or Allah
You are the same, O Lord!
Give every human being
Sanity to perceive this.

Then, in a feeble, husky voice, weakened by his recent fast, Gandhi asked if there were any Muslims in the audience. When he was told that there were none, he shook his head sadly. Gautam wished he had Haseena by his side that Thursday evening. Wouldn't Gandhi have felt redeemed to know that a Hindu, turned Christian, was now committed to marrying a Muslim?

A voice now rose, feeble but firm: 'We have indulged in senseless killings, abductions, forced conversions, and we have done all this shamelessly.'

Everyone could see a glow of righteous wrath in Gandhi's eyes as the evening sun caught his face.

Gautam felt as if the Mahatma had spoken to him exclusively. If only he'd known about Haseena's suffering at the hands of the Delhi pimps! But as for 'forced conversions', in this case it was a voluntary act, though used as a subterfuge to secure his release. Pardonable, therefore.

Nor was his killing of Pannalal senseless. Wasn't that justified too, as a pure act of self-defence?

When question time came, Gautam, troubled by his conscience, stood up to ask if killing was pardonable in certain special circumstances.

'Never', responded Gandhi, 'for the means are as important as the ends, however, worthy they may be.'

'Then why did Lord Krishna exhort Prince Arjuna to kill his own kinsmen on the battlefield of Kurukshetra?'

There was a moment's pause. Gandhi seemed to ponder over Gautam's question.

But before any answer came from the platform, something exploded in the air. Everyone jumped up in fright, except Gandhi, who kept sitting, serene and unruffled, as though the deafening blast was a mere firecracker. In a few minutes, it became known that someone had thrown a hand grenade at the Mahatma from the garden wall, close by. The man was immediately nabbed and handed over to the police. But as he was being taken away, he was heard shouting: 'We'll do it again . . . We'll kill this saviour of the Muslims.'

There was now a commotion all over the place. Out on the street, Gautam and his father heard a mélange of voices:

'Thank God, the Mahatma escaped unhurt . . .'

'You must be another Mahatma,' someone shot back from the crowd. 'Do you know how many of us have been thrown out of the mosques by the government, while our temples in Pakistan are being used as urinals? We have no shelter now . . .'

'I lost my entire property in Peshawar . . .'

'My younger sister was taken away by the Muslim goons, in Lahore . . .'

'And here is this fake saint reciting verses from the Koran!'

'Let's call him Maulana Gandhi, not Mahatma . . .'

'Once he's gone, we'll settle scores with the bloody Muslims—now that their British protectors are not there.'

'We'll turn every mosque in Delhi into a brothel . . .'

It was obviously a group of Hindu fanatics, refugees from Pakistan.

'Maniacs!' Shamlal whispered into his son's ear.

'Devils!' Gautam exclaimed.

But further down the street, they heard a couple of women talking to each other.

'How could anyone kill the Mahatma when he walks about under God's own umbrella?'

'Isn't he our new avatar—after the Buddha and Guru Nanak?'

As Gautam lay in his bed that night, he heard

whisperings in his parents' bedroom. He could catch only some snippets of their conversation.

'It seems Gautam's gone completely under the Mahatma's spell.' That was his father's voice, cryptic though tender.

'God help him . . . I hope he'll regain his sanity.'

'Look, darling, can't you see anything else beyond your rigid orthodoxy?' His father's voice was rather gruff this time. 'Isn't he your child?'

'It seems he's more yours than mine.'

'Come on, my dear,' he said pungently. 'You don't know what love is.'

'Haven't I learnt enough from you?' Gautam's mother quipped. 'Even at this age you won't let me alone.'

'Love's not just that only, silly woman.'

'Won't you let me sleep now?' a yawning voice mumbled, 'I'm tired.'

But, a few minutes later, Gautam heard their bed creaking.

Next evening, he took Berry along with him, instead of his father. He was surprised to see Gandhi back at the prayer meeting right on time, calm and cheerful. This time Gautam decided not to ask him any question—just sit there and drink in every word he spoke. After the usual prayers, Gandhi spoke in a voice that was sombre, deep and resonant: 'If I am to die by the bullet of a madman, I must do so smiling. There must be no anger within me. God must be in my heart and on my lips. And you promise me one thing. Should such a thing happen, nobody will shed a tear.'

As soon as the meeting was over, Berry said to Gautam: 'That guy is a teaser.'

'What do you mean?'

'I felt he was teasing me into thinking—that life was more than just hoarding, that it was giving, sharing, not taking . . .'

'Well, haven't you been a giver too—in your own way?'

'Come on.'

Gautam felt that Gandhi's prayer meetings somehow kept him close to Haseena; he could hardly ever keep her out of his mind. Wouldn't the Mahatma have blessed his decision to marry a Muslim girl?'

As for his mother, he noticed a distinct change in her attitude. Had his father been working on her in his own subtle way? Earlier, she used to get disturbed whenever a letter arrived from Allahabad. But this morning, when she picked up a letter from the mailbox, she beamed.

'From her, I guess,' she said.

'You know it, mom,' he smiled.

Then, hurriedly looking through the letter, he turned to her.

'Here's something for you.'

'What's it? Why don't you read it out to me?'

Gautam began to read out a bit from the letter: 'Don't push your mother. Let her take her own time. One should always be patient with one's mother.'

'Very mature and perceptive,' Gautam's mother now said; then added: 'Most unlike you.'

Gautam just smiled.

'Is she pretty?'

'Very beautiful.'

'When will you bring her to me?'

'Very shortly, mom,' Gautam said. 'And don't forget I love you very much.'

'You flatterer!'

Three days later, Gautam applied for leave and left for Allahabad.

As soon as he reached there, his first concern was marriage—now that both families had agreed.

It was a simple and brief ceremony in Haseena's house, without anybody in the neighbourhood knowing about it, except the qazi. All that Gautam was required to do was to recite the kalma, and adopt a Muslim name. 'Just for form's sake,' Haseena's mother said. Readily, Gautam took the name 'Saleem,' although Haseena didn't look very pleased. So, it was as Saleem that he stayed in their house in Mohalla Kashana. The next day, Gautam sent a telegram to Berry, informing him about the date and time of his train's arrival in Delhi, although he knew that nothing could be certain in those abnormal times.

24

Like a snake of interminable length, the refugee special, with its trail of dull-brown bogies and a massive engine puffing out white hot steam, clanged into the Delhi station. Here, it was scheduled to stop for about an hour to pick up some more passengers, mostly Muslim, before proceeding to Wagah, near Amritsar, the terminal point on the Indian side of the international border. Since these specials ran only twice a week between Delhi and Amritsar, on Sundays and Fridays, hordes of Hindu raiders would prowl about the platforms on these days, looking out for the Muslims migrating to Pakistan. In spite of the armed police posted at all vulnerable points, these assaulters would somehow succeed in stabbing an unwary man, or whisking away a young girl.

On this Sunday, however, there was an unusual police arrangement to guard the train which had just come in from Patna. It had brought Muslims from the eastern parts of India—Allahabad, Lucknow, Kanpur and Agra. As far as possible, the Muslims from a particular city were accommodated in the same compartment so that they might have a sense of camaraderie and collective security. Since these helpless creatures would have found it very risky to get off at any intervening station for food or drinks, the government had made arrangements for doling out packets of food at certain convenient points. Several Muslim philanthropists and secular peace organizations had also contributed generously towards their safe and comfortable journey to Amritsar.

'Let me introduce you to Mr Kelkar,' Berry said, turning to the police officer. 'Of course, you may recognize him . . .'

'Indeed,' Gautam responded, recalling the officer with a touch of leucoderma on his face, the one who had provoked his ire near St. John's.

The officer also felt a little embarrassed to recognize the journalist he'd shouted at after an attempted rape of a Hindu woman.

'How are you, sir?' enquired Kelkar.

'Fine,' said Gautam.

'I should again like to apologize . . .' Kelkar said, lowering his eyes.

'Please . . .' Gautam said, 'no more of that.'

'In fact,' Berry said, addressing Gautam, 'you should now thank him for all the arrangements he's made for you—under Mr Thornton's direction, of course.'

'Thanks a lot,' said Gautam.

'Incidently,' Berry added, 'Mr Kelkar will also accompany you all on this train, right up to Amritsar, with a troop of armed policemen.'

'Thanks again.'

Gautam then looked into the compartment and

beckoned Begum Rahim, Haseena and Salma to come out. After escorting them all to a special waiting room, the officer walked away.

When they were all together in the room, Berry handed over the immigration papers to Gautam, who passed them on to Haseena.

'For the two ladies,' Berry said, his eyes straying towards Salma. He was struck by the remarkable resemblance between the two sisters—the same chiselled features, deep brown eyes, wheatish complexion . . .

As Haseena and Salma were busy looking at the papers, with Begum Rahim almost dozing off in the chair from exhaustion, Berry whispered into Gautam's ear: 'Two hours!'

'There you go again.'

'Annoyed?' Berry murmured. 'I just thought I wouldn't mind taking Salma as my second wife, if Sonali didn't return. Look, even their names alliterate—Sonali, Shyama, Salma!'

'You could have two more if you embraced Islam,' Gautam said, now feeling relaxed.

'Why not?' Berry said, throwing another furtive glance at Salma. 'Would you like me also to come with you up to Amritsar? For protection's sake?'

'No, thanks. It should be a lot safer without you.'

As the guard blew the whistle, Kelkar returned to the waiting room.

'The commissioner has advised you, Mr Mehta,' he said, 'to travel in the general compartment for the Hindus and Sikhs only, so as not to arouse any suspicion.'

'I understand,' responded Gautam.

As the train chugged into motion, there was a sudden outburst of shouting: 'Death to all Pakistanis! Pakistan Murdabad! Kill the bloody Muslims!' But the armed policemen on the platform kept the raiders away from the train.

Only half of the seats in the compartment had been occupied. All the passengers were turbaned Sikhs, holding kirpans in their hands, while their women were dressed in shalwar and kameez. Although the law didn't permit anyone to carry a lethal weapon, the Sikhs had been granted immunity on religious grounds.

Gautam seated Haseena and Salma in a corner away from the door, while he himself sat next to Begum Rahim. He'd already given them Hindu names—while Haseena still remained Seema, Salma was named Durga, and their mother just mataji.

On the seat opposite, right across the aisle, sat a young Sikh couple—the husband was a huge creature, but his wife was a delicate woman who was feeding her little infant, under the flaps of her dupatta.

'How far are you going?' the young mother asked Haseena, pressing her child close to her breasts, a benign look on her face.

'We're going to Amritsar,' Haseena replied.

'To visit the Golden Temple?'

Gautam understood that the woman was looking forward to a long chat. There was, of course, nothing else to see in Amritsar except the Temple.

'Yes,' Gautam intervened, fearing Haseena might somehow slip up. Then, turning to his companions, Gautam rolled out their names, also announcing the relationships: 'My wife, her sister and my mother-in-law.'

The young woman's husband, his eyes flitting from Haseena to Salma, also heard the names. Then, taking off his turban and pressing the pleats of his beard against his chin, he said: 'It wasn't any fun at the Delhi station.'

'Why?' asked Gautam.

'We couldn't get a single Muslim,' he said, his eyes glowering, face tense. 'I don't know why there were so many policemen on the platform today. I couldn't put my kirpan to any use.'

'Oh!' Gautam stuttered.

'We'd have travelled much lighter with a hundred Muslims wiped out,' the man said, caressing his weapon.

'My husband has been thirsting for Muslim blood,' the young mother interjected. 'I wonder if he'll ever be satiated . . . I often ask him if Guru Nanak would have approved of all this killing.'

'Well, he has his own reasons, I guess,' Gautam said, scared of provoking her husband into any argument.

'That's it,' blurted out the man. 'Haven't we reasons enough? What are those bastards doing to Hindus and Sikhs in Pakistan?'

'Yes,' Gautam mumbled, though cursing himself for giving in out of fear.

'My wife is a simpleton,' the Sikh said; then, looking proudly at his child, like a lion eyeing his cub, he added, 'I hope he'll take after me.'

'I hope so,' Gautam said, now pulling out of his handbag an old copy of *The Challenge*, and fanning it out to hide his face.

What perturbed him most was the way this man kept leering at Haseena and Salma.

It was now late evening. The train was speeding up somewhere between Ambala and Jullunder. From there, Gautam thought, it'd be just a couple of hours to Amritsar. In the weird silence and deepening darkness, the engine's occasional whistling sounded like some wraith summoning everyone to the netherworld.

Gautam looked at Begum Rahim, sitting near him, mute and frozen with fright.

'Why don't you have a nap, mataji?' Gautam said, turning to her.

'I'm all right, son. I'll sleep a little later.'

Haseena too was wide awake; only Salma had dozed off.

As Gautam looked about the compartment, he noticed that almost all the passengers were now fast asleep, a couple of them were even snoring. The young Sikh mother had stretched herself on a berth, clasping the child close to her bosom. The only person awake was her husband, his lascivious gaze riveted on Haseena's face.

Gautam heard the continuous rattle of a door handle, which sounded like a band of chained prisoners, clanking about in a cell. As he rose to secure the door, Haseena's mother gently pulled at his shirtsleeve.

'Please keep sitting here,' she whispered, her face ashen.

'All right, mataji,' he said, dropping back in his seat.

For the first time Gautam felt like praying. As a young man, he'd always scoffed at it as man's innate weakness. Man prayed, he then believed, whenever he was broken, gripped by some fear, or was impelled by greed to ask God for some material favours.

But now an irresistible urge seized him. Yes, he must pray for this helpless Muslim family. He closed his eyes and started mumbling to himself: 'Haven't I suffered enough already, O God? I know I've no right to ask anything of you. I have lied and I have killed. But, then, what about your divine grace, your willingness to forgive and bless. I now beseech your help, not for myself but for these destitute women.'

He broke off when the door rattle stopped.

Suddenly, Gautam heard the train grinding to a halt. A few minutes later, the lights went off, followed by loud cries and wailing. All the sleeping passengers, men and women, now leapt to their feet. Panic-stricken, Gautam peered out of the window to see Kelkar dashing along the rail track towards the engine. Looking about himself, he noticed that the tough Sikh was gone.

'It's a raid,' someone cried out from the adjoining compartment.

Then Gautam saw Muslims jumping out of the train, screaming, running helter-skelter, pursued by the raiders who brandished their kirpans, knives and sticks—yelling: 'Sat Sri Akal! Har Har Mahadev!' It was now clear that some gang had ambushed the train in the middle of the night to massacre all the Muslims on board.

The other Sikhs in the compartment also rushed out, unsheathing their kirpans. Gautam was surprised to see their womenfolk sitting unruffled, obviously aware that the attack was directed against the Muslims only.

Gautam heard some voices below his window:

'They'd tied a buffalo in the middle of the track.'

'That's why the driver had to brake to avoid a major accident.'

'It must have been all pre-planned.'

'I'm glad we Hindus are no longer behaving like grass-eaters.'

Gautam now felt some pressure against his body. Turning, he noticed that Haseena's mother had fainted, her head leaning against his left shoulder.

'Mataji!' the young Sikh mother exclaimed; then addressing Gautam: 'Why don't you sprinkle some water on her face?'

'She'll be all right,' Haseena said. 'She's not been keeping too well, lately.'

'Look at my husband,' said the woman, 'he must have joined the gang. Oh God!'

As Haseena's mother came to, Gautam said: 'Why should we worry, mataji? It's our own people doing it.'

'Yes, I know,' she stuttered, slowly opening her eyes.

He'd hardly consoled her when a group of raiders charged into the compartment.

'Any Muslims here?' bawled out a stocky man, brandishing a dagger in his right hand.

'No, please,' the Sikh mother replied. 'We're only Sikhs or Hindus here.'

'Sikhs are all right, but we must know about the others . . .' he paused, his eyes now picking on Gautam. 'Who are you?'

'A Hindu—Gautam Mehta,' he replied, fear choking his throat. 'And this is Seema, my wife, Durga, my sister-in-law . . .'

'Will you stop this naming game?' he growled. 'I was asking only you . . . Understand!'

'Haven't I answered, please?'

'Yes, but we'd have to look you over ourselves,' he said, glaring at Gautam. Then, addressing the other women passengers in the compartment, he added: 'We've caught many Muslims travelling in the general compartments, masquerading as clean-shaven Sikhs or Hindus, or even bareheaded sadhus. These treacherous Muslims . . .'

'But this is a Hindu family,' the Sikh mother intervened. They're going on a pilgrimage to the Golden Temple.'

'Maybe it's just a trumped-up story,' the stocky man said. 'We must get at the truth.'

'No harm in their checking him,' another Sikh woman said, sitting at the far end of the aisle.

'That's it!' grunted the stocky man. 'So, come out at once, will you?'

One of his companions now began to drag Gautam out of the train.

'Please,' Haseena's mother implored, her hands folded, 'spare him! . . . We are Hindus, he's my son-in-law. You may kill me, if you like but . . .'

'There's something shady, surely,' grinned the stocky man. 'Otherwise, why this frantic pleading?'

Gautam knew there was no way out. Terror-stricken, he allowed himself to be taken out, after handing over the immigration papers to Haseena's mother.

'I'll be back soon, mataji,' said Gautam. 'Don't worry. Let them satisfy themselves.'

As they led him deep into a maize field, Gautam looked

about to see other members of the gang attacking the Muslim refugees.

Finding his twenty-odd policemen pitted against a hundred raiders, Kelkar ordered his men to bring down the machine guns, and start firing. As the guns began to rumble in the air, the raiders started fleeing.

Darkness lay all around, thick and heavy, shattered intermittently by the guns booming in the air.

Gautam was taken behind a bush and ordered to undress.

'Come on, man, quick,' barked the stocky man; then, turning to one of his companions, he ordered: 'Rip off his clothes if he doesn't cooperate.'

Blood mounting to his face, Gautam began to undress—first his trousers, then his underwear . . . He felt so sick that he nearly threw up. This, he thought, was the desecration of both his body and soul. He wished he'd been killed instead.

As he stood stark naked, like a pale sacrifice offered to some demon, a flashlight probed his groin—then a rough hand probed him between his thighs.

'No circumcision—he's a Hindu all right,' said a voice.

'You may now dress up,' said the stocky man. 'We had to do it, you know.'

As Gautam started dressing up, the raiders made off, leaving him alone in the maize field.

Moisture welled up in his eyes, blurring everything around. He knew he'd now have to carry this scar on his soul all his life.

Almost limping back into the compartment, as though he'd been grievously wounded in the leg, Gautam felt relieved to see Begum Rahim and the girls quite safe. All the other passengers had also returned to their seats—even the tough Sikh.

Begum Rahim didn't utter a word, nor did the girls, but they understood what he'd been through.

Since the guns had frightened the raiders away, an eerie silence descended upon the place. Then came the guard's piercing whistle. The engine lurched into motion, puffing out jets of white steam into the air. Striding along the rail track on his way back to the guard's van, Kelkar looked into Gautam's compartment.

'Sorry, Mr Mehta,' he said. 'I couldn't see you earlier. I hope you had no trouble.'

'No, Mr Kelkar.'

When the passengers saw the police officer talking so deferentially to Gautam, they felt awed.

The train took about two hours to reach Amritsar. Here, as directed by William Thornton, the local superintendent of police escorted Gautam's party to the international border. By the time they got there, it was already morning, with the sun slowly rising above the horizon.

Gautam warmly thanked Kelkar for all his help.

'Will you, please, also convey my gratitude to the commissioner?' said Gautam.

'I will,' he said, and jeeped away.

It was an unending ant line of Muslim migrants, trudging close upon each other's heels. Some of them were carrying only a handbag or a small suitcase, their sole movable property to be carried across the border. Famished and wrinkled faces stared blankly into space. Occasionally, a child whimpered for food or drink, only to be shouted down by his or her parents. As the line moved forward, at a snail's pace, some started up a conversation with the others, sharing memories of what they were leaving behind—their ancestral homes, their friends and their relatives. They were not certain what awaited them in the new country. It was a journey into the unknown.

At the end of the line was the immigration checkpost, which looked like a customs barrier. It had been set up on the southern edge of a bamboo bridge, across a river which drove a discreet wedge between the outskirts of Amritsar and Mumtazpur (a small village on the Pakistani side).

As Salma and her mother inched forward, Haseena and Gautam walked alongside, nobody saying anything. They heard only the buzzing of their thoughts, like bats flapping their scaly wings in the dark.

The die had been cast and there was no going back.

The Pakistani immigration officer scrutinized the papers of Begum Rahim and Salma very closely; he then ushered them across the border, smiling like St. Peter at the gates of heaven.

But before Haseena's mother took Salma across the bridge, she turned back, leaning tearfully over the bamboo railing.

'God willing, we'll meet again,' she cried out, 'Inshallah.'

'Inshallah!' Gautam responded.

Haseena stood mute. Tears welled up in her eyes and her lips and hands quivered. Then she waved to her mother and sister.

Another cry wafted across the bridge:

'Khuda Hafiz! God be with you!'

'Khuda Hafiz!'

Gautam and Haseena stood on the southern bank of the river, waving to two shadowy figures, gradually fading into the crowd on the other side. Then they were gone, as though sucked into some whirlpool.

Gautam took Haseena's hand gently into his right palm, looking deep into her eyes.

'I love you,' he breathed.

'I love you too,' Haseena's voice was a mere whisper; then dovetailing her fingers into his, she mumbled: 'Now, call me Haseena Mehta.'

'No, my love,' he said. 'Not Haseena Mehta.' Then, carried on the crest of some powerful emotion: 'Just Haseena Gautam—our first names only . . . Yes, we'll start a new race—sans caste, sans religion, sans nationality.'

Their handclasp deepened into a warm pressure; a current flowed from one body to the other.

As Haseena leaned her head against his shoulder, he caressed her hair. Then, looking at both sides of the river, he saw the same chequered fields of maize. He wondered if the long drooping ears of their stems also heard the mute cries of the displaced, who walked across the bridge every day.

The sky was now covered with mountains of clouds—white, inky blue and grey. They assumed all sorts of fantastic shapes—of giant dinosaurs, their long necks craning forward, of the skeletal remains of some primordial mammals, of an army of soldiers on the rout. Ceaselessly, they sailed across the bridge, from India to Pakistan, casting fugitive reflections in the tawny waters of the river.

Suddenly, a flock of birds shot into the sky, and began to circle joyously over the maize fields on either side, as though scornful of the happenings on the earth below.

Their spangled wings, poised securely against the wind, glimmered in the morning sun. Their puny belly tanks charged with some inexhaustible fuel, they flew round and round, up and down—and warbled.

Acknowledgements

I am grateful to Amitendu Bhattacharya, my young friend, who has helped me with proofreading and editing.

A Note on the Author

Shiv K. Kumar has donned many hats and lived many lives: poet, novelist, short-story writer, playwright, translator, academic and critic. He was born in Lahore, where he received his school and college education. He obtained his doctorate in English Literature from the University of Cambridge. Prof. Kumar has published thirteen volumes of poetry, five novels, two collections of short stories and a play. His poems have appeared in several renowned newspapers and journals like the *New York Times*, *Poetry Review* (London), *Western Humanities Review*, among others—and been broadcast on the BBC. In 1978, he was elected a Fellow of the Royal Society of Literature (London). He received the Sahitya Akademi Award in 1987 for his collection of poems *Trapfalls in the Sky*. In 2001, he was awarded the Padma Bhushan for his contribution to literature.

A Note on the Type

Sabon is the name of an old-style serif typeface designed by the German-born typographer and designer Jan Tschichold (1902–74) in the period 1964–67. A distinguishing feature of the typeface was that the roman, italic, and bold weights all occupy the same width when typeset—an unusual feature, but this meant that the typeface then only required one set of copyfitting data (rather than three) when compositors had to estimate the length of a text prior to actual typesetting (a common practice before computer-assisted typesetting).